HER ALIEN CYBORGS

SUSAN HAYES

The only thing that ever came easy for her was trouble.

After a lifetime of busting her ass and bending the law just to scrape by, Hezza is running on fumes. Her ship is even older than she is, and both are feeling their age. Is she ready to retire? Hell no. Hanging up her flight suit is the last thing she wants, even if it's the smart thing to do.

Before she can make that choice, though, trouble finds her again... and this time it comes with a double order of hard muscles, sinful smiles, and alpha attitude.

They had nothing. No past. No future. No names. Then she appeared... and everything changed.

Subjects Six and Seven are failed experiments. Created in secret using banned technology and stolen DNA, they were crafted as weapons for a not-so-distant war. Too stubborn to be controlled and too valuable to terminate, they exist only to serve... and to dream of freedom.

Fate brought three battered hearts together, but it will take more than luck to survive the coming storm. Hezza is their key to happiness, and the cyborgs are her first rays of hope in a life spent in the shadows. Together, they're going to change the galaxy... or die trying.

This book is dedicated to Craig. For all you are. For all you do. For saying "I do." For being the hero in my own love story.

PROLOGUE

Beyond the edge of civilized space is a newly colonized planet. It's a haven for the homeless, the hopeful, and those dreaming of freedom.

The beings who live here might be different species from vastly different worlds - but they all have one thing in common. Whoever they are, and wherever they came from, Haven is now their home.

The land is uncharted. The dangers are unknown. It's a world full of possibilities – for those willing to risk everything.

Welcome to Haven Colony.

CHAPTER 1

Hezza leaned back in her chair and let her eyes close most of the way.

To really sell the idea that she was relaxed and indifferent to what was happening, she made a conscious effort to slouch down in her chair as far as the restraints allowed.

The pair of overzealous dock security dipsticks had cuffed her hands and feet to the chair. Not only that, but they'd placed her in a room with bare plasteel walls, a floor liberally covered in mysterious stains, and three shabby, dented metal furnishings. One was the chair she sat on. The other two were a table with a matching chair on the far side. As far as she could tell, all of it was bolted to the deck to prevent the inhabitants from what? Throwing it at the walls? Using the chair as a weapon? Probably both.

This was the kind of place where you housed a dangerous fugitive, and there wasn't a snowball's chance in a supernova she fit that description. It was strangely flattering but hardly an accurate assessment. She was a smuggler, not a killer. The only things she was capable of murdering were fried foods and ice cream.

The thought made her smile, which she had no doubt the cameras would catch and display to whoever was watching her. Someone *would* be watching. They always did. Anything she said or did now would be tossed back in her face once the questions started. She knew how the game was played. This was the waiting period, when she was left on her own to marinate in her fear. No one would show up until she was tenderized and compliant. At least, that's what they taught the rent-a-cops in places like this.

Carnax was like every other back-system station she'd visited. They barely broke even on refueling contracts and providing replacement parts to any ship unlucky enough to break down this far from civilized space.

She wasn't here for fuel or repairs, though. She'd been here for a job. It was supposed to be a simple in-and-out cargo pickup—easy work, no fuss, no muss, and no questions asked.

Looking back now, she probably should have asked some *fraxxing* questions, starting with who had made the request in the first place. When she got out of here, she'd have a long, colorful chat with Sasha. Either he was getting sloppy, or he'd been paid to set her up. Either way, she'd make sure his reputation as a broker tanked after this.

If she got out of whatever-the-void trouble this turned out to be. For the moment, all she knew was what security had told her. She was being detained for acts in violation of the Unified Galactic Agreement. Which was normally corporate speak for, "We'll let you know what the charges are once we've determined how many credits worth of fines you can pay."

This time, though, things felt different. Like maybe she was in serious trouble.

Hezza had to remind herself to stay relaxed as she pondered what this could be about. She'd always preferred to bend laws instead of breaking them completely. Sure, her current cargo included a few items she hoped port-sec didn't inspect too closely. The embryos in the cargo pods were marked as domestic chickens destined for a colony world. However, odds were good they were something far more exotic, expensive, and only available on the black market.

Moving illegal cargo didn't bother her, so long as it didn't break one of her rules. She didn't transport slaves, drugs, or weapons. Every broker she used knew this. Of course, most of the brokers she knew were already retired and enjoying a life of leisure, likely funded through years of skimming profits and pocketing bribes.

Now that she thought about it, most of her friends were retired too—some by choice, yet others because they'd be incarcerated for the rest of their lives. As far as she was concerned, there wasn't much difference. Both meant staying in one place and doing the same thing day after day. No thank you.

The problem was, she couldn't keep flying cargo forever. She wasn't slow, but the *Desperate Gambit* couldn't keep up with the newest ships out there. Both she and her ship were losing business to younger, hungrier pilots.

She slumped deeper into her chair. *Getting old sucked.*

Three minutes later, Hezza told herself to quit wallowing. She had more immediate problems to deal with. She went over the list of probable reasons she was in custody. The most likely cause was also the easiest to understand. No good deed went unpunished.

River was a decent being who'd had more than her share of suffering. The cyborg had come to her with money in hand and a contingency plan in case things went sideways.

Turned out, things hadn't just gone sideways. They'd gone full nova. River's contingency plan had kicked in, and Hezza made sure the cyborg made it to her chosen destination. Had she broken a few laws to do it? Yes. Would she do it again? *Abso-fraxxing-lutely.*

That didn't mean she had no regrets. Things had gotten messy. Edge, the grumpy, self-appointed leader of the cyborgs, had demanded Hezza reveal where River had gone. Then the damned fool had gone after her. One cyborg leaving the colony was a problem. Two? That set off all kinds of panic. Various factions had learned of her involvement, and she'd had to lay low.

Apparently, she hadn't laid low enough. A message from River had caught up with her a few days ago. The good news was that she and Edge were fine and had handled the asshole hunting River. The bad news? The fallout from their actions was still ongoing. Nova Force was still looking for Hezza, and it would be best if she stayed out of sight for the time being.

If she'd been smart, she would have taken the warning more seriously. She should have gone dark and drifted somewhere in the big black. Instead, she'd gotten cocky and assumed no one could find her.

Hezza uttered a sigh. Given her current situation, it was apparent someone *had* found her. That left her with two questions. Who had set this trap, and what did they want?

Odds were good she wasn't going to like the answers.

She had no way to check the time, but it had to have been more than an hour since someone had made an appearance.

She'd been listening for footsteps outside the door to her cell or at least a click as they let themselves in. Instead, she heard a low, electronic hum followed by a soft chuckle.

"That does not look comfortable," a familiar voice drawled.

Hezza's eyes snapped open, and she straightened in her chair. "Phylomenia Harrington, what the *fraxx* are you doing on my wall?"

The silver-haired woman on the monitor laughed. "*Your* wall? Did you take over the port security office already?"

"I could have, but they gave me some pretty bangles, so I've decided to behave." She raised both wrists as far as the cuffs would allow, to show off the restraints.

"*Qarf.* They weren't supposed to do that."

Phylomenia turned to glare at someone out of view. "Did you tell them to restrain her?"

"I told them she was a potential flight risk," a deep male voice replied.

"And you wonder why people distrust those in authority. *This* is why, Scott Archer. You and I are going to talk about this."

Archer. Hezza felt like she should recognize the name, but nothing popped into her head. Phylomenia had left the life a few years back. Whoever this guy was, she must have met him after she went straight.

"So all of this is your fault," Hezza stated. It had to be true, but it made no sense. Phylomenia was not exactly a friend, but they'd been in the same orbit most of the time. She was someone whose word you could trust, and they'd had a few laughs and drinks over the years.

Phylomenia gave her a rueful smile. "All of it? No. You got yourself into this mess, Hez. I'm here to offer you a way out."

"From what? No one here will tell me what I'm charged with."

"That's because they weren't given the details. And you're not under arrest. You're being detained for questioning." Phylomenia arched a brow. "And don't tell me you don't know what I'm talking about. You helped not one but two dangerous cyborgs escape from Haven colony."

That made her laugh. "They're no more dangerous than anyone else you and I have done business with. Hell, they're a lot better than some I could name."

Phylomenia's eyes narrowed. "You didn't just help them out for money? You actually *like* these cyborgs?"

Hezza raised her head and stiffened her shoulders in response to Phylomenia's tone. What did the woman have against cyborgs?

"They're decent beings who got a raw deal from the day they climbed out of their maturation vats. So yeah, I like them."

"Enough to help one get off the planet she was legally required to stay on, and to hell with the consequences?" Phylomenia asked.

"Keeping them on Liberty was a bullshit call that should never have happened. As for what I did? It wasn't about the money. River needed help, and there wasn't a snowball's chance in a supernova that anyone from the corporations or the military was going to step up. It was about doing the right thing."

She leaned forward as far as her restraints would allow. "Was a time you'd have done the same thing. What changed?" It wasn't the question she should have asked, but it was out of her mouth before she could reconsider.

Instead of the rebuke she expected, Phylomenia's expression softened, and she chuckled again. "Sorry, Hez. I needed to be sure you were on the right side of this mess. I didn't change, but you could have, and that would mean you're not the one we need right now."

"I heard a lot of words, and none of them told me a damned thing. What in the void is going on, Phyl?"

The woman on the screen gestured with both hands, and two men joined her. They were older but still fit with neatly trimmed gray hair and a physical presence that screamed of military training.

"These are my husbands, Scott Archer and Garrett Michaels. Archer negotiated the original deal with the Vardarians for Liberty."

"They got the planet for colonization, but they had to take the cyborgs the rest of the galaxy was too scared to deal with." Hezza knew the story. "Which means he's the *bakaffa* who made it so none of the cyborgs could ever leave."

She intentionally used the Vardarian insult to remind the others of her ties to the colony. Her daughter and her mates all lived in Haven.

"It was necessary at the time," one of the men said. She assumed he was Archer.

"And it was never intended to last forever. You know what corporations are like, Hez. Everything is a negotiation. They wanted to try for more before agreeing to anything else."

"How much longer will they be stuck?" Hezza asked.

Archer answered, "That's being discussed right now. I can't give you an answer because I'm retired and out of the loop. But it won't be long. Too much has happened."

Well, that was good news. It didn't explain what they wanted with her, though. "I'm glad to hear it. Now what does this have to do with me?"

Phylomenia's expression turned stormy. "There's another research base. The Interstellar Armed Forces are sending a small fleet to investigate. Scott called in some favors and got us added as consultants. It's not that we don't trust them to make the right call..."

Hezza understood immediately. "They're military, which means they're going to make decisions based on their training."

The other man grunted in agreement. "To a hammer, everything looks like a nail."

Scott Archer shot the man a dirty look. "I'm not a hammer, thank you very much."

"But sometimes you're a tool."

Phylomenia sighed. "Please ignore them. Their idea of flirting leaves a lot to be desired."

Hezza grinned. "It's kind of cute. I still need to know why we're having this conversation, though. And I'd really like to get out of this chair."

"Here's the deal, Hez. We're going on this mission, but we can't interfere too much. We're just advisors. We need someone who can *do* something if things go nova."

"You want me along as your backup plan. I'm interested, but I still don't understand how you're going to convince the IAF to let me tag along."

"That's easy. This is likely to be another cyborg research and development station. The cyborgs of Haven have requested representation on this mission. Since none of them are allowed to leave the planet yet, they've designated someone to speak for them."

"Me?" Hezza nearly choked on the word.

"You," Phylomenia confirmed with only a hint of a smile. "The job's yours if you want it."

She couldn't turn down the offer or the honor it represented. Still, she did have a reputation to live up to. "I'm interested," she said, trying to sound casual. "But first I need to know. What does this gig pay?"

CHAPTER 2

The muscles in his arms burned as his shoulders felt like they were about to tear loose from their sockets, but he kept going.

"Four hundred," he announced as he reached the milestone.

"How is that possible? I'm matching you rep for rep, and I'm only at three hundred and eighty-six." His companion shot him a disgusted look from the other side of their cell. "If you're going to cheat, try not to be so obvious about it."

"I'm... not... cheating," Fyr'enth said, adding a rep between each word. "You... can't... count."

Bickering was another way to alleviate the boredom, and it took less effort than the vertical push-ups they were doing.

Burning off energy wasn't easy when they spent most of their time confined to a cell. In the beginning, it hadn't been like this. The days had been filled with combat drills, weapons training, and a litany of tests designed to gauge their physical and mental toughness.

Back then, the entire cell block was full of beings like them. Test subjects, their creators called them back then. Now? They were referred to as failures.

Fyr'enth understood why they saw him that way. Physically, he and Kalan were exactly what their creators envisioned. In test after test, they'd proven themselves to be the strongest and fastest. The other subjects were good, but the two of them were better.

Their bodies weren't the problem. It was something about their minds. They fought their programming and found ways around their orders. It was the same for all the others.

Over time, the assessments piled up, and the entire cohort was declared a failure. Now he and Kalan were the only ones left. Even some of the ones created after them were gone. Why was he still alive? He had no idea, but in the quiet times, it gnawed at the corners of his mind. Better to stay busy.

"Do you think they'll feed us today?" Kalan asked, his tone as pointed as his fangs. Every word they spoke, either aloud or via their implants, was monitored. The question wasn't intended for him. It was a shot at whoever was listening and a reminder that even cyborgs needed to eat occasionally.

He managed another five reps before replying. "Hungry already, Seven? It's only been three days."

Officially, they didn't have names. Seven was the first digit in his companion's identification number. He was Six. They'd chosen names for themselves more than a year ago, though it had been months before they'd had the opportunity to tell each other what they were. In a life of constant surveillance, every element of his world was controlled by someone else. The thoughts in his head and his name were the only things that truly belonged to him.

"Even experiments have needs, and I'm not getting most of mine met."

While he didn't disagree, Fyr'enth wasn't interested in antagonizing their creators. That inevitably led to punishment of some sort.

"We're alive," he reminded his clone. While they were almost identical in appearance, their personalities differed. He was the quieter of the two while Kalan seemed to thrive on conflict. Since they'd been together from the moment they'd left their maturation vats, it had to be something in their behavior programming. Not that either of them understood exactly what had been done to them. All they knew was what they'd been told or managed to glean from overheard conversations.

Kalan grunted as he pushed off from the wall and righted himself. "Alive, yes. Also bored, hungry, and bored. Yes, I said it twice." He raised his voice to a shout. "Because I'm bored!"

Fyr'enth got to his feet too. There wasn't much point in continuing to exercise. Their nanotech would keep them in peak shape even if they did nothing but eat and sleep all day. He knew that because it had been one of the few experiments he'd endured that hadn't involved some form of torture.

"Remember the time they made us do nothing but eat and lie around for two..."

The rest of his sentence was cut off by the blare of alarms.

"*What the* fraxx?" Kalan sent through their implants.

"*No idea,*" he sent back. "*But it's not a fire drill.*" They'd heard that alarm every month. This was something different, and different usually meant trouble.

He dealt with the noise by decreasing the sensitivity of his hearing. The sonic bombardment continued for ninety seconds before finally ending. The lights continued to strobe, so whatever the problem, it wasn't resolved.

Kalan paced like a caged animal, his agitation obvious. Fyr'enth felt the same way, but he remained still and waited.

A few minutes later, they both heard the buzz of the security hatch activating. Kalan pivoted to face the sound, his entire body tensed with anticipation.

Fyr'enth stayed where he was. Why waste energy? The door was locked, the bars still as solid as they'd been a moment ago. Whoever it was, they were still in control.

For now.

The footfalls were soft and hesitant, giving away their visitor's identity before they took more than a few steps.

"Hello, Ansari. Why are you here?" he asked.

"Hello." The female's voice was as soft as her footsteps. "I can't stay long. Things are happening out there, but I needed to do this."

"Do what?" Kalan stood at the bars, his gaze locked on the Pheran female. She was the only one of her species on the research station, and her duties were unknown. She wasn't a technician or one of the medical staff. She came around only occasionally, usually with food or some kind of entertainment for them.

Her wide silver eyes were bright with fear. "Someone's coming here. To Orio Station. We've been ordered to leave. They're destroying the files right now." She raised one blue-furred hand, palm up, to show them a data stick. "But I have this. It's all I could get, but it should help."

"Help with what? Who's coming?" As far as he could tell, she spoke the truth. Nothing in her body language or even micro-expressions indicated otherwise. The lack of details was annoying but no reason not to believe her.

"Interstellar Armed Forces. That's what I heard anyway. No one knows for sure. We're abandoning the station. There's no time for the other contingency plans. The ships are almost here already."

She glanced back toward the door. "I have to go. Please understand that I never wanted to be part of this. They bought my contract..."

Fyr'enth sensed she was about to bolt. "You have always been kind to us. Thank you for that."

Kalan reached through the bars, his hand open. "Give that to me and go. You don't want to be left behind."

Tears glittered in her eyes as she moved closer. "I do, though, but if I tried..." She shook her head. "I don't want to die, either."

She tossed the data stick to Kalan. "Live well. I wish I had done more."

She turned and fled, but not before he saw her tears. Were they for herself? For them? He didn't know. He didn't understand what she'd meant, either. Live well. What did that mean?

He was still mulling everything over when Kalan broke the silence. "I got to say, that was not what I expected." He held up the data stick. "Tears, kind words, and a goodbye gift from the only being on this station I don't want to kill."

"What do you think is on that?" he asked.

"Evidence," Kalan said, his voice flat. "Hopefully, it includes an explanation of what the *fraxx* they did to us. Maybe some of it can be undone."

"Like the behavior mods?"

Kalan nodded. "Yeah. It would be nice to know that I'm making my own choices instead of some decision-making matrix they hard-coded into my head."

"If they had complete control, we wouldn't be classified as failures, but I know what you mean. Most of the time we can't be sure our choices are really *ours*."

Kalan lapsed into silence, his gaze locked on his hand. "Do you think this is another experiment?"

"No," he said, confident in his answer. Ansari's fear, and her tears, were very real.

"Do you think the IAF will treat us better than these *bakaffa* did?"

Fyr'enth considered the question for several minutes before giving his answer. "I think the enemy of our enemy could be our friend."

"I like that." Kalan slipped the data stick into the pocket of his pants. Like everything else in the cell, their clothes were an indeterminate gray color, cheaply made, and well-worn.

Fyr'enth pointed toward the sanitation area. It was just a tiled patch of floor with a drain and an overhead shower fixture. The only privacy they were allowed was a two-meter-high partition that screened off the toilet area.

"I don't know about you, but I'm going to get cleaned up. Might as well try to make a good first impression."

His clone scoffed and ran a hand through his too-long beard. "I think that ship left orbit already."

He toed off his boots and stripped down while he talked. "That's on you. The last time they let us have scissors, you tried to stab that asshole guard with them."

"I didn't try. I *did* stab him. Twice."

"Fine. You tried to kill him," Fyr'enth clarified. "You failed, which is the only reason we're still alive."

He walked over to the tiled space and activated the shower. The water was little more than a tepid drizzle, but it was better than nothing.

"If we're lucky, whoever finds us will let us have long, hot showers."

"And real food," Kalan said. "I never want to see or smell another bowl of algae broth ever again."

They lapsed into silence after that, both of them pondering what this change in fortune might mean. Would they finally be free? Or were they about to exchange one set of bars for another? There was no way of knowing and nothing to do but wait.

Whatever the future looked like, he hoped it was better than this.

CHAPTER 3

When she'd agreed to come along on this mission, Hezza hadn't expected high-octane adventures and action scenes. That was the stuff of holo-vids, not reality. The military loved their procedures even more than they enjoyed shooting things, but she still hadn't been prepared to be this painfully, utterly bored.

For starters, the *Gambit* wasn't fast enough to catch up with the rest of the task force on her own, so she'd been parked inside a hangar of a much larger military vessel for the trip. Hezza had taken advantage of the opportunity to do repairs and maintenance on the old girl without needing to don an EVA suit. Once she'd joined the others, she'd assumed she'd be back in the cockpit.

Wrong.

The leader of the task force refused to allow it, citing some ridiculous regulations and claiming that civilian pilots couldn't meet the same standards as their military counterparts. It would have stung more, but the stuffed-shirt colonel insisted that Archer's ship had to be transported, too. Given that both Phylomenia's husbands were former fighter pilots, no one on either the *Desperate Gambit* or the *Bat Out of Hell* had been happy.

They'd bonded over good booze and bad jokes at Barrios's expense, but not even decent company could alleviate the boredom. In the end, she'd spent most of her time upgrading the *Gambit*, using parts and equipment involuntarily donated by the IAF.

Arriving at Orio research base had allowed for some excitement, but watching everything unfold through relayed broadcasts quickly got old. Most of the ships had already evacuated before the task force was in range. One was destroyed, and another captured, but so far, there had been no information on who or what was on board.

Annoyed by her own thoughts, Hezza opened a channel to the *Bat*. Phylomenia's face appeared on the monitor almost instantly.

"Sorry to ask, but have you heard anything?" Hezza asked.

"Not a *fraxxing* thing. Scott's ready to go nova. He's not used to being kept in the dark."

"Why bring us all this way if they're going to treat us like mushrooms?"

Phylomenia snorted. "Damn good question. Scott has sent some messages. Hopefully, someone with rank will find out what's going on and lodge a well-polished boot up the colonel's ass. The whole reason we're here is to provide informed guidance and ensure that any cyborgs still on the station are dealt with properly. How can we do that if we're stuck in this hangar?"

"I don't like it. My gut is telling me something's

happening over there, and they don't want us to know until it's too late to do anything about it."

"I agree. Let me talk to my husbands again. It's time to stop playing nice."

That made Hezza laugh. "About time. I was starting to wonder if you were going soft. I hear marriage and retirement can do that to a person."

Phylomenia flicked out two of her fingers in silent insult. "You don't know what you're missing. Seriously. I wouldn't go back to my lonely life for all the scrip in the galaxy."

She waved the other woman's words away. "Don't curse me with your bad luck. I'm happy with my life exactly the way it is."

Was it a lie? Yes. But if she repeated it often enough, maybe she'd believe it was true.

"You keep telling yourself that. In the meantime, be ready to move. They can't keep us off the station forever."

"I'll be right here, waiting for something to happen."

The call ended, leaving her with nothing to do but stare at the console of her flight controls. Habit had her back in the cockpit despite the fact that her ship was docked. This was where she spent most of her time and was the one place where she felt like she was in control of things... even when she wasn't.

"I hate waiting," she muttered, tipping her chair back far enough she could comfortably rest her feet on the corner of the console. After two minutes, she was back on her feet, too keyed up to sit still.

For the next two hours, she kept herself busy with small, simple tasks she could drop at a moment's notice.

Hells, she'd even swept the cargo bay, despite the fact her small fleet of servo-bots kept the ship immaculate already.

When her comms chimed, she had to bite back a whoop of relief before answering. A brief glance told her it was a recorded message sent from the bridge of the *Bright Arrow*.

Finally.

The message was audio only, but Barrios's tone made it very clear he was not pleased. "The Orio research base has been secured. You and the other civilians are now invited to enter and begin your part in this mission. As all military craft are currently busy, you are instructed to use your own ship as transport. Coordinates and docking codes are attached to this message. Colonel Jonathon Barrios. Out."

She turned on her heel and hurried to the cockpit of her ship. "It's about damned time."

Of course, that wasn't the end of the waiting game. The moment she'd set foot on Orio Station, a pair of soldiers had approached and escorted her to an empty room for a briefing that never happened. No doubt the other group were getting the same treatment, but someone had been smart enough to keep them separated. That didn't stop them from using comms to stay in touch, but apart from a few tidbits Archer had managed to pry loose from their guards, they were still being kept in the dark.

All she knew was that the captured ship had several inhabited cryo-pods on board. One of the newly captured prisoners had stated that the beings inside were all experimental test subjects.

They had to be cyborgs, which meant she should be involved. Instead, Barrios had arranged things so that she'd rushed to Orio Station just as the cryo-pods were moved onto the *Bright Arrow*.

She'd been played, and she wasn't happy about it.

After waiting for half an hour or so, Hezza decided she'd had enough. Since she was on the station now, it was time to start poking around to see what she could find. After a lifetime of hiding contraband, she knew exactly where to start looking.

She went to the door with a story prepared about needing to use the facilities, but to her surprise, there were no guards. That made things easier. Since they'd brought her in from the right, she turned left. A lifetime spent walking the corridors of countless ships and stations gave her a rough idea of what the most likely layout should be. Usually, the upper decks were command and control with the middle decks designated for residential use—housing, dining areas, and on larger stations, even entertainment. The lower decks would be where the real work was done. In this case, that meant laboratories and offices. She intended to go lower still, down to the bottom decks. If any of the test subjects were still on the station, that's where she'd find them.

The easiest way to avoid getting caught somewhere you weren't supposed to be was to act as if you had every right to be there. She walked with purpose, her head up and her steps measured. The ID badge they'd given her to wear while she was on the *Bright Arrow* was clearly visible. They were on the same team, and she was just doing her job, the same as everyone else.

She ran across only one other group of soldiers on the way. They saw her ID, made the assumptions she hoped they would, and passed by with nothing more than a nod of acknowledgment.

The route she took kept her away from the core of the station, which meant it took her longer to get where she wanted to go. The layout wasn't quite what she'd expected, either, but eventually she found what she was looking for.

This part of the station felt emptier than the other areas. The corridor lighting was dimmer, and the only noise was the hum of machinery hidden behind heavily reinforced bulkheads. There were no markings on any of the doors, and the usual navigational aids were all missing.

This had to be the right place.

Someone from her side must have gained access to the station's controls because every door she passed through was already unlocked and open. Every door but one.

At the end of one corridor was a reinforced hatchway that spanned the width of the hall. The keypad beside was backlit with red lights, a sure sign it was locked.

That meant whatever or whoever was on the other side must be important. Why else would it be excluded from the standard opening command?

She took her time examining the keypad. It looked like countless others she'd seen in her life. Whoever had built this place hadn't bothered with a high-tech system that scanned hands or retinas. This relied on users knowing the correct access code. She was no hacker and had no idea how tech like this worked. What she knew were people. And everyone, every species she knew of, shared some common traits.

She checked the bulkhead around the keypad and found what she needed scrawled in uneven characters to one side of the device.

She chuckled as she tapped in the code. "Thank you for confirming my theory that no one wants to remember another *fraxxing* passcode."

Despite her curiosity, Hezza stayed put until the hatch was completely open. No sense rushing toward potential trouble.

Beyond the heavy hatch was another corridor, but this one was different. Instead of unmarked doors, this area had cells, complete with thick metal bars.

Jackpot.

She held up her comm device and captured several images. Then she sent a quick, encrypted message to Phylomenia that included the photos and her approximate location. Only then did she enter the new area.

"Hello?" she called out in Galactic Standard. It was common knowledge that cyborgs were programmed to understand and speak every known language, but why make it complicated? Galactic Standard was exactly as the name declared, a standardized language used by all the known species.

"Are you from the IAF?" The voice was low, deep, and male.

"Sort of. They're here, and I came on one of their ships, but I'm not military. I represent another group."

"Explain." The voice sounded the same, but something told her it wasn't coming from the same being.

She raised her hands, palms out, and moved toward the voices. "My name is Hezza. I'm here because some friends asked me to come. I think you and they probably have a lot in common. They were kept in a place like this once. They're free now, though, and they want you to know you aren't alone anymore."

"Why would they care about us?"

She reached the front of the cell and turned to face the inhabitants. She'd been about to explain that her friends were cyborgs, but the words died unspoken.

She'd met cyborgs before. Plenty of them. But these two were nothing like the others. For one thing, they weren't based on human DNA.

"Oh *fraxx*. You're Vardarian." She eyed the two captive males in disbelieve. This was not at all what she'd expected.

It was so much worse.

The pair were identical, so much so that she assumed they were clones. Both were large and heavily muscled, which was typical for cyborgs. They had silver scales, with the familiar barcode style marking on their wrists. Every cyborg she'd ever met had one. Apparently, the assholes running this research base hadn't felt the need to change their identification protocols when they'd added a new species to their research.

They were Vardarian, no doubt about it, though she'd never seen any look quite this... primal. Their dark blond hair and beards were long and wild, as if they'd never met a barber before in their lives. Given their situation, that was probably true.

She considered them for a heartbeat and then two. Her first impression was that the two were viscerally beautiful and more than a little feral. She'd have to be careful.

"We're not Vardarian," one of them said. He stood next to the bars of his cell, his gray-blue eyes locked on her.

"We're cyborgs," the other continued. He stood in the back corner of their cell with his massive arms crossed over an equally huge chest. "We're not the same species as our donor DNA."

That was interesting. The cyborgs she knew saw themselves in the same way. They referred to themselves as cyborgs. Never as humans.

"The beings I represent are cyborgs, too. They care because they're the same as you in some ways, and they would like to offer you a safe place to recover." She gestured around them. "From all this."

The one closest to the bars stiffened, his head snapping up to stare at the door. "Someone else is coming. Several beings, and they're in a hurry."

Veth. She needed more time. Would closing the hatch slow them down? Probably not. One of them would think to look for the passcode, just as she had.

"They're IAF soldiers. They won't hurt you, but they'll likely shout orders and try to boss you around. Me too. Do me a favor and stay calm. I have friends on their way. We'll get this sorted out."

She took a deep breath to center herself. But instead of helping her focus, her pulse sped up, and a sudden rush of heat washed over her.

She ignored it.

Instinct told her she needed to put herself between the two captives and the incoming soldiers. She moved before she could consider the ramifications, placing herself less than a meter outside the bars, and then turned to face the hatch.

"What are you doing?" the nearest male asked.

"Giving them a reason to stop and think before they do something stupid."

The male growled. "You would risk yourself for us?"

"Apparently," she said, only paying partial attention to what she said. Most of her focus was on the hatchway and the hammer of boots on the deck.

The first soldier came through the door a few seconds later, their weapon already trained on the two in the cell behind her. The combat armor and helmet made it hard to be sure, but she thought it was a woman.

"Ma'am, you need to step away from the prisoners. Now." The soldier's voice was amplified through her helmet's speakers.

"I'm not moving," Hezza said in her calmest, most rational tone. "At least not until you stop pointing that weapon at me and my new friends."

The response was not what she had hoped for. Instead of relaxing, the group of soldiers tightened their grips on their weapons, and the few who hadn't raised their guns to the ready position did so.

Fraxx.

She opened her mouth to protest, but instead of a rational statement, all she uttered was a startled yelp as a barrier of metal snapped out in front of her. She tried to push her way clear, but it closed in around her, forcing her back against the bars.

It took her baffled brain a few seconds to understand what had happened. The metal wall surrounding her was actually a *wing*, complete with overlapping strips that reminded her of feathers.

She couldn't see the soldiers, but she could still hear them.

Several were cursing while the woman who had spoken before shouted.

"Let the woman go. Taking a hostage isn't going to help you."

Hezza snorted. This one was even worse at diplomacy than she was. "I'm not a hostage, and the only ones causing issues are all of you. You're on a *fraxxing* rescue mission. Remember? We're here to save these beings not threaten them."

The room went silent for several long seconds, and then the woman spoke again. "Point taken, ma'am. Everyone, lower your weapons."

"Thank you," Hezza said. Then she twisted herself around to face the cyborg who had shielded her. "You need to let go of me."

"No." The male's voice rolled through her like a sonic boom. She craned her neck until she could see his face. Well, not really, because his beard obscured most of his features. She could see enough, though, to know he was angry and more than a little confused.

Without thinking, she reached up and smoothed her fingers across the furrows in his brow. The moment of connection hit her like a comet strike. Her heart raced, her knees went weak, and a sense of pure, unadulterated *need* tore through her.

"What is this?" the male demanded. "What are you doing to me?" His wing tightened around her, pressing her against the bars of the cell.

"You're crushing me," she protested. "Let go."

"Not until you explain." He inhaled deeply, his nostrils flaring as heat began to burn behind his eyes.

"Yes, explain." The other male moved into view. "Why do you smell like that?"

"Like what?" she asked, confused for a second. Then understanding dawned. Hell's bells and gravity wells. Seriously?

Hezza didn't know whether to laugh, cry, or curse. For a long moment she stared at the two males and then burst out laughing. "*Fraxxing* really? Now? Them?" She directed her questions to the universe at large.

"Why are you laughing?" the first male asked.

"Answer my question," the other demanded.

"I'm laughing because if I don't, I'm going to swear until the paint peels off the walls." She let her gaze move between the two males as she struggled to find the words to explain.

"Did your captors ever tell you about something called the *sharhal*?" she asked.

They both looked at her with blank expressions. That would be a no. Alright then. Nothing for it but to fly straight at the truth and hope to survive the impact.

"The *sharhal* is the Vardarian word for it. We humans call it a mating fever. It happens when your species meets someone who shares the same biochemical signature. Or something like that. I'm not an expert. It's not something we can ignore either. If we go too long without uh, dealing with these feelings, it can do serious mental and physical damage."

She opted to gloss over the fact that it likely meant the three of them were destined to be lifelong mates. She really was not ready to face that possibility. There had to be a way to undo this. She didn't want mates, and these two deserved a chance to enjoy a real life before settling down with a female. Preferably one their own age.

"You want to mate with us?" the closest one asked.

She really needed to learn their names. It seemed like the least she could do, all things considered.

Names first. Then... She slammed the brakes on that line of thought. That was a problem for later. They had other issues to deal with first. Preferably before the annoying colonel showed up and made things worse.

"What the hell is going on here?" a new voice demanded.

Of course, it was Barrios. With her luck? She'd probably summoned him like a mythical creature just by thinking of him.

"You need to lower your wing and let them see me before someone does something stupid." As she spoke, she reached up to grasp the top line of his wing. Even using most of her weight, she couldn't make it move.

Frustration and worry replaced the other more carnal

thoughts dancing through her head. "Please. Only enough for them to see my face."

That did it. The wing lowered enough for her to see the group crowded into the corridor. Some of the soldiers had moved back to allow Barrios and several others to take their places.

"Hey, Phylomenia. Look what I found."

The other woman shot her a rueful look. "I should have remembered that was one of your talents." Phylomenia turned to look at her husbands. "She always did have a knack for finding trouble."

Hezza glanced back at the two males standing behind her. Trouble didn't begin to describe the situation. It was a *fraxxed-up* mess with no easy solutions and a biological clock that had already started ticking.

She needed to get these two out of their cell and somewhere safe before anything else went wrong.

The way this day was going, Hezza figured she had about five *fraxxing* minutes until that happened. Maybe less.

CHAPTER 4

Kalan bared his fangs and glared at the beings outside the bars. If any of them tried to hurt *her*, he'd kill them in the most violent, painful ways he could think of. It didn't matter that she was a stranger. This female was *his*.

She said her name was Hezza. That was all he knew, and it was enough. At least for now. Soon, he'd want to know more. More about her and about this thing she called the *sharhal*.

Was this really his mate? Their mate? It had to be something like that because he was almost out of his mind with the need to touch her.

"Do you feel this same madness?" he asked Fyr'enth.

"Yes, but I don't understand it. I know her. Need her."

"And would die to keep her safe." He finished the thought. They'd been linked like this from the beginning. It wasn't telepathy, but sometimes it felt like it.

Kalan drew in another breath, letting the scent of the female—their female—flow into his mouth and nose. She smelled sweet, like the candy one of the techs had snuck to him as a present once. He wondered if she'd taste like that illicit treat, too.

"Ahem." Someone made an annoying sound that tore Kalan's attention away from Hezza. A human male stood in front of the others with his chest puffed out as if he were trying to make himself look bigger.

"I am Commander Barrios. As the commanding officer of this task force, I am taking control of this situation. You will release the civilian woman immediately. Both of you will then move to the back of your cell and place your hands on the wall at shoulder height or higher. Do you understand?"

"No," Kalan said.

The little man spluttered. "No? No, what? Do you need me to use smaller words, or are you disregarding my orders?"

Hezza spoke up. "The only ones under your command are *your* soldiers. Unless they signed up while I wasn't looking, these two don't need to follow your orders."

"They are my prisoners. Of course, they have to follow orders." The leader glared at Hezza.

Kalan glared back, and a soft growl of warning rose from his throat.

"It's okay, sunshine." Hezza patted the top of his wing. "He's not going to hurt me."

Her touch soothed him, but he didn't let it show. Everyone here was a potential threat, and he would not show weakness.

"If I could make a suggestion?" Another male spoke.

This one had gray hair and carried himself with quiet authority. Not like the other one.

"Yes, yes. Of course you have an opinion, *Mister Archer*."

Kalan didn't understand why, but the first word sounded like an insult.

The one called Archer nodded. "Thank you, Commander Barrios. Given the situation, it might be best if you sent your people off to continue clearing this level. Their presence is complicating the situation. I can assure you that Hezza is in no danger."

"Are you insane? One of them is holding her hostage!"

Kalan snarled. "I am holding her, yes. As a hostage? No. I am protecting her from all of *you*."

A female spoke up. She had silver-white hair and a sardonic smile. "Do you understand what the *sharhal* is, Commander? Because I do. Hezza is quite safe. It's the rest of us you should be worried about. They will protect their *mahaya* from any threat, and right now? You're the ones pointing weapons at her."

Mahaya? It sounded like a word he should know, but he'd never heard it before. Nor was it in his language files. He didn't recognize the word *sharhal* either. How many other words and concepts had their creators hidden from them?

"What is this word?" he demanded.

Hezza turned to look at him, and he noticed her eyes for the first time. They were deep green with flecks of brown and gold near the center. "It means mate."

That he understood. "You want to mate with us?"

She laughed at that. "It's more complicated than that, but let's hold off on explanations until we can be alone." She turned to glare at Barrios. "Because this situation is none of the IAF's *fraxxing* business."

The male huffed and stiffened his spine. "That is your opinion. I see this matter differently. You were instructed to wait in a safe location while the station was cleared. Your refusal to follow directions has resulted in a hostage situation. Since your judgment is obviously flawed, I will be making the decisions from now on. The two males will be secured and taken to the *Bright Arrow* for medical assessment and debriefing. All civilians will be escorted off the base and back to their ships."

Archer slashed his hand through the air and moved to stand in front of Barrios, deliberately blocking his view. "Commander Barrios, you lead the military component of this task force, but not the civilians. That's my responsibility. We're here to do a job, and as far as I can tell, you are actively preventing us from accomplishing our mission."

He lowered his voice to a gentler tone but continued without letting Barrios reply. "I've seen the *sharhal* before, Commander. That particular event resulted in chaos, disorder, and the Dynamex corporation losing an entire planet to the Vardarians. I imagine you would not want a repeat of that situation to play out here."

Kalan might not be able to see the officer, but the male's waspish tone told him everything he needed to know. "You're the expert. Of course, I will consider your recommendations. I will also remind you that I am responsible for the safety of the entire task force, including you and your group."

Archer nodded. "Of course. Which is why I'm recommending we de-escalate this situation by having your soldiers leave the area."

"This is all going in my report."

Kalan smiled a little. He knew a surrender when he heard one. Archer had won this round.

Barrios ordered the others to leave, though he lingered near the still-open hatch.

"Close the door on your way out if you would?" Archer asked, his point as sharp as a well-honed blade.

The other female hid a smile behind her hand, but her eyes twinkled with amusement. That, more than anything else, made him open to the idea that these might be allies of a sort.

Maybe.

"It's safe now. You don't need to shield me anymore," Hezza told him.

Her light tone and relaxed body language confirmed her words. She wasn't concerned. Not even about him.

That was a first. Everyone on the station had treated their creations with wariness. Some refused to even look at them, and even those who had demanded certain intimate services had never been entirely at ease.

He retracted his wing through the bars but slipped an arm around her waist to ensure she stayed close to him. He wasn't interested in letting her go. Not yet. Not while every cell in his body screamed with need.

It pleased him when she simply rested one warm hand on his forearm. She stroked him gently, her fingers tracing small, pleasurable patterns across his scales. The caress heated his blood and made it hard to think clearly.

"So, this got complicated," she drawled. "Any suggestions?"

"Let us out of this cell," Fyr'enth said.

Archer held up a hand. "We'll do that, but first I need some information. Starting with your names and why you appear to be the only two subjects still on the station."

"I'm Seven," the answer came automatically. Then he remembered that the circumstances had changed. "At least, that's what our captors called me. My chosen name is Kalan. What are your names?"

"I'm Scott Archer. That is Garrett Michaels, and this is our wife, Phylomenia." Archer made introductions and then looked at Six, who had moved close enough to rest a possessive hand on Hezza's shoulder. "And your name?"

"I was called Six. Now I would like to be called Fyr'enth."

Hezza turned enough to be able to smile at both of them. "Hello, Fyr'enth and Kalan."

Kalan went still and stared at her for several seconds. It was the first time in his life he'd heard his name spoken by someone else. They'd told each other their chosen names only once and never said them aloud again.

Not until today.

The one called Garrett ended the moment with another question. "Do either of you know why you were left behind?"

He tightened his grip around Hezza's waist before answering. "They left us here because we have no value to them."

Now she knew the truth, he expected Hezza to pull away. Instead, she leaned back against the bars that separated them as if offering him her silent support.

"No value?" Archer asked.

"We are failed experiments," Fyr'enth explained. "If we're the only ones left, the others were terminated. We thought as much, but we had no way to be certain."

The three humans shared a knowing look with each other, but Phylomenia spoke first. "Let me guess. They wanted you to be completely obedient at all times with no free will. When you resisted, they deemed you failures."

It was not a question, but Kalan replied anyway. "Yes. How did you know that?"

"Because that's what always happens. These people —we call them Shadows—have tried this more than once. It never worked. I guess they decided to try it with a different species this time."

"Is that why you were surprised by our appearance, Hezza? Were none of the other cyborgs based on Vardarian DNA?"

"The others are all based on human genetics," she said. "As far as we know, you're the first. The empress is going to shed her scales when she hears about this."

"That's a future problem," Archer said. "Let's focus on the issues facing us in the here and now."

Hezza nodded. "Like how to get these two off the station and away from Barrios. He's got his own agenda, and I don't trust him."

"Neither do we," Phylomenia said.

"Nor us," Fyr'enth stated with a hint of a growl. "He wants to separate us from Hezza. That will not happen."

"It won't," Hezza reassured them. "You're staying with me until we get this *sharhal* thing sorted out."

Archer nodded. "As much as it pains me, I agree. As for getting you off the station? I have an idea."

Garrett chuckled. "You've been waiting for a chance to use that thing."

"Smoke and mirrors?" Phylomenia asked.

He had no idea what they were talking about. Nor did he care so long as it meant they wouldn't have to be here much longer. After years of waiting, it was finally time for action.

"We're really leaving," Fyr'enth said via their link.

"We are." He glanced down at the female still in his embrace. *"And the universe has provided us with a guide."*

"I think she's a great deal more than that, brother."

"I do, too." He wanted to believe that, but when had the universe ever given them anything? If this was a gift, it had to come with strings.

CHAPTER 5

An hour later, Hezza was ready to scream in frustration. They had a workable plan, but it wouldn't work if Barrios would not agree to let the two cyborgs out of their cell.

"Security on my ship is my call, and I'm not allowing those two on board unless they are restrained and have an armed escort. My brig can hold them until they can be assessed and debriefed." The commander had repeated the same line three times in as many minutes, and she wanted to smack him for it.

"That was never the plan," Scott retorted. "Any prisoners we recovered were to be provided with housing and medical support. We even agreed on which deck would be designated for their use. There's no reason for these changes."

"There's every reason. Those two are not like any cyborg we've ever encountered. We have no idea what they're capable of or why they were left behind. I will do whatever is necessary to protect my crew. Either they go into cryo-pods, or they have to be restrained." Barrios folded his arms and nodded as if this would end the argument.

"That can't happen. If you separate them, there is every likelihood that the two cyborgs will go insane and possibly die," Phylomenia chimed in.

The arrogant little *wapiti* shrugged as if this was not a concern. "Then they should go into cryo. From what I understand, that should slow the mating fever down."

"But you don't know for sure," Hezza countered.

"Of course I don't. This is another species we're talking about. Which is why I intend to return them to Vardarian space, eventually."

"Eventually is not good enough," Archer said. "They should be free to go now."

"We don't even know if the empress will accept them. Hells, you haven't asked what *they* want." Guilt hit hard the moment those words left Hezza's lips. She hadn't asked them either. The two big cyborgs paced behind the bars of their cell, listening to the argument without comment.

Fraxx.

She turned away from the others to face the two males. "I'm sorry. We're talking about your lives and not even including you in the conversation. Fyr'enth and Kalan, what do *you* want?"

"I want out of this cell!" Kalan snarled.

"And to get far away from this place," Fyr'enth said. "We told you already. We are not Vardarian. This empire you mentioned has nothing to do with us. Why send us somewhere we have no desire to go?"

All three of them were agitated as they dealt with the situation and the *sharhal*. The longer they were in the same room, the more intense things got. At this point, she had to fight the urge to stand next to the bars just to be closer to them. Thinking was almost impossible because her head was full of erotic images of what she wanted to be doing right now and what she wished the two young males would do to her.

Barrios huffed. "This is ridiculous. I won't be dictated to by a group of civilians and a couple of *machines*."

She was in his personal space less than a second later, glowering down at him with one hand clenched into a fist at her side. "Cyborgs are not machines. They're living beings."

"That is your opinion. Some of us see things differently."

The opportunity was too good to pass up. Was this how they'd planned it? Not by a light-year, but they hadn't expected Barrios to be this difficult.

This might be their best chance, so she took it. "In that case, there's no way these two are going on your ship. They will stay with me on the *Gambit*. That way your precious ship and crew are safe from them, and they will be safe from you."

Scott shot her a sour look but stayed silent.

Barrios turned a satisfying shade of crimson, spluttered, and had to take several deep breaths before he spoke again. "Unacceptable!"

Fyr'enth joined the conversation before anything else was said. "We agree to this proposal."

That simple statement filled her with an unexpected

sense of warmth and acceptance. This stupid *sharhal* thing was even worse than she'd been told. How was she supposed to function like this?

"Commander Barrios. Given your personal feelings about cyborgs, I have to agree with Hezza's suggestion," Garrett said. He had more wealth and influence than the rest of them put together, and Barrios knew it. He also knew he'd *fraxxed* up by saying what he had.

Two seconds later, he caved. "If it means keeping those two off my ship, I'll agree to it. But!" He raised a finger. "I insist they be escorted to the civilian's ship by six of my soldiers. And all of this is going into my report."

"We will also be submitting a report," Scott said. Then he looked at her. "Hezza will put together a list of supplies she'll need. I'm happy to transfer the goods from the Bat and then request replacements from your quartermaster once we're back on board." His lips quirked up into a brief but dangerous smile. "After all, the cyborgs are guests of the IAF. Their care and comfort are your responsibility, Commander Barrios."

She managed to hide her amusement and keep a straight face, but it wasn't easy. "Of course. I'll have that for you by the time we get to the ships. It won't be much, just food, sundries, and a supply of raw materials for producing clothing and anything else they need."

Barrios went a darker shade of crimson but only gave a terse nod.

"Could we let our guests out of their cell now?" Hezza asked, her voice as sweet as syrup.

Another nod.

"Thank you, Commander." She turned toward the

two cyborgs and finally let herself smile. They were one step closer to freedom. Now...came the hard part.

True to his word, Scott arranged for several crates of goods to be transferred to her ship. His ship's AI was more advanced than the one on her vessel. It accepted his directions and had everything packed and waiting before they reached the shuttle bay, where both ships were parked.

She sent instructions for her ship to send out the cargo droids to collect everything, and just like that, she had everything they would need for the next part of the plan. The bit where she flew like hell to get away from Barrios and anyone else who might be a threat to her new charges.

While she was worried about them, they seemed more concerned about her safety. The moment the cell door opened, they'd taken up positions on either side of her, both of them extending one wing to shield her back. Later, she intended to ask about their wings. They were not the standard for their species. Instead of a membrane stretched over their bone structure, these looked more like the wings of a bird, complete with metallic feathers.

They'd stayed quiet and watchful for the entire trip back up to the hangar deck. Now that no bars stood between them, they were impossible to ignore. Even if she hadn't been hit with the mating fever whammy, she suspected she'd have enjoyed looking at them. Attractive wasn't a strong enough word, and beautiful was too gentle a description. They were mesmerizing.

Kalan and Fyr'enth walked with purpose, their gait carefully measured to match the smaller humans around them. Despite the restriction, they moved like predators.

Part of her knew it would be wise to be wary of them, but she wasn't. Even stronger than her physical attraction and hormone-fueled urges was a sense of security and *rightness* that was as unsettling as it was unfamiliar.

It took an alarming amount of effort to drag her attention off the pair of cyborgs and back to reality, but she managed. Mostly. The soldiers were already turning away when she tripped over the threshold of her own blasted entry hatch. Kalan caught her hand to steady her, and she allowed herself to enjoy that brief touch longer than she should have. With a mental shake, she let him go and turned to close and seal the hatch.

"Computer, secure all cargo for hard maneuvers, and confirm that all hatches are closed and sealed."

"Hatches are sealed. Cargo is being secured now." The flat, sexless voice of her ship's AI stated.

"Good. Once that's done, have the bots prep both passenger cabins for..." She looked at her companions and did some quick thinking. They would need a lot of space. "Prep the cabins for Torski-sized passengers. Oh, and prepare for launch."

"Tasks registered and in progress."

With that done, she turned to face the two cyborgs. "Fyr'enth and Kalan, welcome aboard the *Desperate Gambit*. I'll show you your quarters and give you the grand tour once we're safely on our way. For now, please come with me."

She gestured down the corridor toward the cockpit and led the way there. "I don't suppose either of you has flight training?"

Fyr'enth only shook his head, but Kalan spoke up. "We have ship-to-ship weapons training, but no piloting skills."

"That makes sense. Why teach your prisoners anything that might help them escape?" she said.

"Exactly," Kalan said. "Will you teach us?"

That was an easy question to answer. "I'd be happy to. It'll help us pass the time. We're weeks away from anything that resembles civilization."

"And the more civilized an area, the more likely that someone like Barrios will be there, looking for us, so we'll be keeping to the fringes?" Fyr'enth asked.

"I've got a few places in mind." They'd touched on that topic during the planning stage, but only in general terms. The less Phylomenia and the others knew, the better.

They reached the cockpit, and she slid into her seat. "One of you can squeeze into the copilot's seat. The other can take the gunner's chair. Strap in and don't touch anything. We're about to find out if the parts I *acquired* from the *Bright Arrow's* inventory are as good as I think they are."

"Acquired?" Fyr'enth asked.

"You stole them?" Kal said with what she thought was a hint of approval.

She laughed. "I prefer to call it creative acquisition, but Barrios would definitely call it stealing."

Kalan grinned widely enough she saw his fangs. "So, we are escaping that *bakaffa* using parts you stole from his own ship?"

"That's the plan."

"I like this plan," Kalan said.

The two of them went quiet, and she assumed they were having the same sort of internal conversation the cyborgs she knew in Haven sometimes had. After a few seconds, Fyr'enth claimed the seat beside her while Kalan tried to fold himself into the gunner's chair.

If they were still alive and in the clear after this, she'd have to make some changes to the ship's layout.

A little voice piped up from the back of her mind, reminding her that the size of the chairs was the least of her problems. Adjusting the ship was easy. Accepting that she might have just experienced the alien version of a shotgun wedding? That was going to take some work... and a cargo crate full of chocolate.

The launch protocols were almost complete when she got the call. Phylomenia's face filled the monitor, an easy smile on her lips.

"You ready?"

"We're all settled in and ready to launch. Barrios sent over instructions on where he wants us. It shouldn't be a problem." The entire conversation was a performance, but they both played their roles. It was meant to give Phylomenia and her group cover and make it look like they had no idea what was about to happen.

"We'll talk once we're underway. Just wanted you to know we're ready when you are."

Hezza nodded. "Then I'll get out of your way. Enjoy your time on the *Arrow*. I'll keep you updated."

The screen went black, and two seconds later her comm chimed.

Every message sent this way was heavily encrypted and undetectable over short distances like this.

"Hello again," she greeted her friend.

"Scott's ready. The effect should hit every vessel in the vicinity, but he's not sure for how long. You'll have to be fast."

"We'll manage. Thank you for everything. The invitation to come on this mission, and for well, everything. Same goes for your men. They're not bad for a couple of military types."

"Take care of yourself and your new mates. We'll make sure the other cyborgs are safely delivered to Haven. Barrios is a biased, wrong-thinking idiot, but I don't think he's working for the Shadows. Even if he is? We'll see this through."

"We will," she agreed, ignoring the part of her mind screaming in panic about the easy way Phylomenia called them her *mates*. "When you get to the colony, tell Anya the first round of drinks is on me."

Phylomenia laughed at that. "Your daughter will be the one who needs a drink when I tell her what's going on."

"True, but it's her bar. I'm not paying for *her* drinks. She can buy her own."

Archer said something off screen, and Phylomenia's

expression turned serious. "It's showtime." She raised a hand in a gesture of farewell. "Fly faster than your troubles, my friend."

Hezza mirrored the gesture as she completed the old smuggler's refrain. "May good fortune be your copilot."

She secured her comm and flexed her fingers over the controls.

"We're out of here," she said without looking back. "Welcome to freedom, you two. Brace yourselves; this next bit is going to be fun."

CHAPTER 6

Fyr'enth wasn't sure what to expect now that they were ready to depart. His only experience with space travel had been in combat simulations and training to familiarize them with troop transports and dropships.

At first, it all seemed the same. The engine noise increased in volume, the deck beneath his feet started to vibrate, and then the ship rose off the hangar deck. If anything, it was smoother than the virtual experience.

Hezza was obviously an experienced pilot because she made it look easy to maneuver in the relatively tight space. He stared at the viewscreen as the massive doors slowly opened, revealing the unending expanse outside.

A shimmer of energy pulsed across the gap.

"What is that?" he asked and pointed at the viewscreen.

"A force field. It allows the hangar bay to stay pressurized even when ships are entering or leaving the area. It takes a lot of power to maintain, so most stations only activate them when the doors are open.

That made sense, though it made his scales tighten to think about the cold and deadly void beyond those doors. It was a clear reminder that freedom came with new dangers.

The three of them stayed silent as they passed through the energy field. Then Kalan exhaled sharply as if he'd been holding his breath. "We're free," he said in a voice tinged with awe. "We're actually free."

"Hold off on the celebration for a bit longer," Hezza said. She was focused on her instruments, her jaw set and eyes narrowed.

The seconds stretched out as they waited for the next phase of the plan to kick off.

Fyr'enth tried to enjoy every moment. If things went badly, this might be his only taste of freedom.

"What's taking so—" Kalan's question was cut off as a cacophony of noise erupted around them. Alarms screamed, lights flashed, and the viewscreen lit up with dozens of red dots.

"And away we go!" Hezza whooped. "Ship, initiate Rapid Exit Protocol, and turn off those *fraxxing* alarms!"

He had no idea exactly what that protocol entailed, but apparently it included shutting down the ship's artificial gravity. Fyr'enth's stomach lurched as the ship rolled down and away from its previous course. It also felt like it was pulling away from *him*, with only his safety harness keeping his ass in the chair.

He grabbed the straps across his chest and looked over at Hezza. She laughed as she put them into a spin.

She thought this was fun? Their rescuer was crazy and a *fraxxing* good pilot.

The fleet of nonexistent enemy ships flooded the *Gambit's* sensors, which was exactly what they'd hoped for. Barrios's ships should have the same problem. The sheer number of potential targets made it possible for Hezza to slip away unnoticed.

It was the best plan they had, but it wasn't without risk. Archer couldn't be sure it would work on multiple ships at once. The device was a gift from someone Archer had claimed was a better hacker than the "pink-haired princess of chaos."

He had no idea who that was or how something on board Archer's ship could affect so many other vessels. They hadn't had time for questions, and he suspected he wouldn't have understood the answers anyway. He and Kalan had made the difficult choice to trust Hezza and her companions.

When he'd imagined a future where he was free to make his own decisions, trusting his life to a stranger hadn't been on the list.

"Ship! More power to the inertial dampeners, or we're going to need to scrape ourselves off the deck plating with a spatula," Hezza said. Her smile didn't waver, but her tone was deadly serious.

He looked at her again, this time seeing beyond her easy smile. Her hair was short and neat at the sides with bangs that swept across her forehead. He'd initially thought her hair was white, but now he saw there were still traces of red and copper in it.

Fine lines showed around her eyes and the corners of her mouth. How much they showed changed according to her expression. She was not as thin as some of the female techs he'd seen on the base, but the flight suit she wore made it impossible to judge much more than that. He thought she was above average height for a human female, but compared to him, she was small.

He watched as she piloted. The ship's movements were surprisingly agile and easy given it was a freight hauler. At one point, they doubled back toward the station and then dove beneath it, flying so close to the station's hull he felt like he could reach out and touch it.

The radio was almost as chaotic as the viewscreen with various voices demanding sit-reps and explanations while others tried to provide information that was lost because they talked over each other.

"This is the vaunted might of the Interstellar Armed Forces?" Kalan sent via their link. *"They can't even manage basic comm discipline in a crisis."*

"I doubt they sent their best on this mission. Barrios might have the rank of commander, but he seems like the administrator type. I think some of the sims we watched called them desk riders?"

Kalan barked out a sharp laugh before answering. *"Desk jockeys."*

"Right. My point stands, though. He can't be a top-tier officer. Archer is. Or he was."

"Agreed."

The babble of voices finally stopped when Barrios spoke. He must have used some kind of override because everyone else went suddenly silent. "This is Commander Barrios. What is happening? Lieutenant Commander Heath, what is the status of the *Bright Arrow?*"

A new voice entered the conversation. This one younger and female. "Sir, this is Heath. According to the Arrow's sensors, there's an enemy fleet in the area, but we're not seeing anything on our viewscreens. They're ghosts, sir. I can't explain it."

Hezza chuckled. "I would love to see how Barrios spins this in his next report. Do you think he'll blame little green men?"

Fyr'enth frowned as he tried to make sense of her question? "I'm not aware of any alien species that fit that description."

That made her laugh harder. "Sorry. Earth joke. Way back before humans left their original solar system, there were legends about alien visitors. Some of them were about little green men."

Some of the vids and books he'd enjoyed involved the myths and stories of other cultures. Mostly human, but some had been Torski and Pheran as well. He'd wondered why they never let them view anything about Vardarians. Now he realized it was to ensure they didn't discover the gaps in their knowledge.

Another minute passed as they raced for open space, putting as much distance as possible between themselves and the other ships. Hezza used the ghost ships as partial cover, flying from one phantom image to another to avoid notice.

Even with the inertial dampeners at maximum, the ride was far from comfortable. Every change in direction or velocity exerted a noticeable amount of force. One second he'd be forced deep into his chair, and the next he was floating as the safety straps dug into his chest and shoulders. The chair itself was not designed to accommodate his wings, so both he and Kalan had draped their wings over the back of their too-small seats.

Once they passed beyond the range of Archer's light show, Hezza stopped the acrobatics and poured on the speed. She wanted to put as much distance as possible between the *Gambit* and any pursuers before engaging the FTL engines.

For reasons he didn't understand, the calculations needed to navigate hyperspace included knowing the ship's precise position the moment the engines activated. If they were out of position by so much as a meter, they could pass too close to a star and be torn apart by gravitational forces. Hezza explained the key points as they sped toward the coordinates chosen by the ship's AI.

"Please begin deceleration. Failure to do so will result in our overshooting the coordinates."

Hezza grunted in annoyance. "I don't tell you how to do your job. You don't tell me how to do mine."

"You are incapable of performing the calculations required to carry out my function," the AI replied. Its tone remained neutral, but there might have been a hint of sass in the response.

"That's beside the point." Despite her complaints, Hezza toggled the thrusters near the front of the ship in order to reduce its velocity.

"Ideally we'd come to a full stop before spinning up the faster-than-light drive, but these are not ideal circumstances." She patted the console in front of her.

"The AI doesn't have much of a personality, but it makes up for it with raw computing power. We'll be fine. I've done this..." She chuckled. "More often than I care to admit."

"You've rescued research subjects like us before?" Fyr'enth asked.

"Hells no. This is a first. I meant that in my line of work, it's sometimes necessary to get gone in a hurry."

"I thought you were a freighter pilot? Why would that require you to make escapes like this?" Kalan asked with open curiosity.

She turned to flash them both a wicked smile. "I said I flew cargo. Truth is, a lot of what I carry isn't exactly legal." She waggled one hand back and forth. "Not illegal, either. Usually. Most of my work is somewhere in the murky gray area."

"You're a smuggler," Fyr'enth said without judgment. Everything she and the others had done to get them away from the IAF probably fell somewhere in that same gray area. All that mattered to him was that she had risked herself for them. It was more than anyone else had ever done.

"I am." She shrugged and faced forward again. "It pays the bills."

"And it saved our lives," he told her. Instinctively, he placed his hand on her shoulder. She leaned into his touch, and that small interaction filled him with a deep longing that eclipsed the lust he'd felt since the moment they'd met. He wanted her, yes. But he wanted *more*, even if he didn't understand what that meant.

"This female..." Kalan didn't finish the sentence. He didn't have to.

"She has the heart of a warrior," Fyr'enth sent back.

Kalan's reply carried a tinge of amusement. *"Her heart isn't what concerns me. The life she lives, the way she flies. Do you think she's sane?"*

He turned to smile at his brother. *"I hope not. I, for one, do not wish to be mated to some soft, gentle female who could never understand who and what we are."*

It took several long seconds for Kalan to reply, and when he did, his words were uncharacteristically measured and thoughtful. *"Do you really believe she is our mate?"*

"Maybe. How else do you explain what is happening to us? She believes it, and her physical reactions to us cannot be denied. I can smell her desire."

"So can I," Kalan agreed. *"And it's testing my will far beyond anything they did to us back on Orio."*

"Same for me. I have never craved a female like this before. My cock aches. My scales are tight and tingle in the strangest way. I want to hold her in my arms, bury my head in her hair, and drink in her scent."

"Me too, brother. And so much more than that. Do you think she will say our names when we make her come? I would like that."

A mental image of that scene made his cock twitch and his balls tighten. He'd like that too. Very much.

The seconds ticked by too slowly, but eventually they made it to their destination. Hezza pulsed the thrusters again, slowing them down as much as she could.

"Ship, activate the FTL drive when ready," Hezza ordered.

"Activating."

He'd experienced this many times in simulations, but the transition to light speed still caught him by surprise. Total darkness encompassed the ship. In the lightless void, there were no visual references at all, which made it impossible to judge their speed or even tell if they were moving.

"Weird, isn't it?" Hezza said. "I know we're moving faster than light right now, but I bet your senses insist we're stationary."

"It is unsettling. In training sims, it always felt like we were in motion."

"They probably do that to make it feel more realistic, even though it's not accurate."

Hezza glanced over the instruments and then exhaled deeply. "No one followed us in. That's good. We'll have to drop back into normal space, change course, and then jump again a few times over the next twenty hours or so. That should make it difficult for them to follow our trail. They'll probably find us eventually, but I won't make it easy for them."

Now that they were safe, she relaxed. Not by much but enough for her mask to slip. He saw the signs of stress and fatigue. Her voice was softer now, and the lines around her eyes seemed more defined. The adrenaline must be wearing off. His nanotech kept his body's chemicals carefully balanced to avoid the kind of crash Hezza was experiencing.

"Do you need to rest?" he asked.

She shot him a look that made him wince. Apparently, he'd said the wrong thing.

"I do not need a nap. I'm not *that* old."

"Why is your age relevant? We have all been under stress. Now that the threat level has lowered, your body is purging itself of the chemicals that kept your senses elevated. We have nanotech to manage that sort of thing. You do not."

"Ah." Her expression softened. "Sorry. I thought you were implying..." She trailed off and shook her head. "Never mind. I was wrong, and I apologize. It *has* been a long *fraxxing* day."

Her words stunned him into silence. No one had ever apologized to him before. He stared at her. She stared back, not with judgment but with understanding. It made him feel seen in a way he'd never experienced. Like he was more than an object to be used. Like he *mattered*.

Eventually, Hezza undid the fastenings on her chair and got to her feet. "I think it's time I showed you two to your new quarters. Ship, run continuous sensor sweeps and inform me if anything, including a fleck of space dust, appears somewhere it should not be."

"Affirmative," the AI responded.

"And now I'll give you the grand tour. It won't take long. Most of the *Gambit's* interior is dedicated to cargo space." She eyed them for a moment before nodding to herself. "Since I don't have much cargo at the moment, it should give you both somewhere to stretch your wings and fly. I bet that's not something they let you do very often."

"It was not," Kalan said. "Thank you. That would be..." He paused before finishing his sentence. "Nice."

Hezza laughed and raised both hands, palms out. "Don't start saying things like that. I have a reputation to protect. I'm a veteran of the void with a cold heart and a bad attitude."

Then she winked at them. "If you think otherwise, kindly keep it to yourselves."

CHAPTER 7

Hezza took them around the ship, showing them the various levels and areas. She even gave them a brief tour of the engineering deck. She didn't want them to feel like she was keeping anything from them. Eventually, they'd make their way back to Haven colony and get all the education and support they needed. For now, she was all they had.

They deserved better.

They asked her questions while they walked the decks of the *Gambit*. They wanted to know about Haven and the beings who lived there. She'd told them about the colonists, both the Vardarians and the cyborgs, and how the two groups were blending into one. That led her to tell them the story of how her daughter had met her Vardarian mates.

"So this has happened before?" Kalan had asked as they made their way back to the main level. "Between our species and yours?"

"The *sharhal*? Yes. When Archer mentioned the

event that resulted in chaos and Dynamex losing a planet? That happened the first time our species made contact. The human involved is named Phaedra, and she lives on Liberty with her *mahoyen* and their daughter. One of her mates is the leader of the colony and a member of the royal family. His sister is the empress."

"Empress Neha's brother rules this colony?" Fyr'enth asked.

She noted that they knew about the Vardarian empress but nothing about the colony. Someone had carefully controlled what they knew, and that was never a good thing.

"One of the leaders, yes. There's a ruling council with representatives from every species. They just had their first elections to select more members. A few stepped down, and other spaces were created to make sure everyone has an equal voice."

"That sounds fair and reasonable." Kalan scowled. "Which is not something I expected from members of the royal family."

And there it was. Hezza stopped and turned to face the two males. "I hate to say this, but I think you need to question a lot of what you've been told. The Vardarian empire is far from perfect, but I know the prince personally, and he's a good, decent male who cares deeply about the colony and everyone in it. From what I've heard, his sister is less open-minded, but she's not some evil tyrant. Since we're on the topic of trustworthiness, what were you told about the corporations?"

They answered in perfect sync, their delivery so

perfect it gave her chills. "The corporations are the caretakers of human-occupied space. They improve the lives of the citizens while ensuring prosperity for all."

Then Kalan snickered. "Or that's what we're supposed to think. We've viewed enough vids and books to know the truth. They're greedy, soulless, *bakaffas* with no interest in improving anything but their bottom line."

Relief washed over her. They needed more information, but they weren't brainwashed. "You scared me for a moment there. Yeah, you've got it right. Though not all of them are complete assholes. A lot of them are run by beings like our friend Barrios. They focus on following the rules and keeping things nice and tidy. They're happy to slap a coat of paint on top of all the suffering and shit and call it a day."

They reached their final destination in comfortable silence. They were probably processing everything that had happened today. She wasn't talking because it took too much effort. All she wanted was a hot shower and a cup of cocoa with marshmallows. Instead, she planned to take a cold shower and down a dangerously large mug of *ja'kreesh*.

That should be enough to snap her out of her lust-fueled fugue. She wouldn't sleep for a day or so, but that was fine. She had to stay up for the next nineteen or so hours, anyway. She'd rest once she was sure they were safe.

"These are your quarters." She pointed to a pair of doors set across the passage from each other. "Nothing fancy. I don't have crew or passengers on board that often, but you should be comfortable. There's a bed, a vid screen, and a sanitation room attached to both cabins. That reminds me. Ship, you listening?"

"Always."

"Good. I need you to add the males with me to the ship's roster. Their names are Kalan and Fyr'enth."

"Spelling?" the ship asked.

She smiled at them. "Tell the AI how you want your names spelled."

They gave her matching bemused looks and did as she requested.

"There we go. Ship. Mark them as crew and give them full access to all standard systems. Oh, and assign them the standard pay and benefits package."

"Done."

They stared at her, disbelief and confusion on their faces. "Access to all systems?" Kalan asked.

"Pay and benefits?" Fyr'enth said.

She wasn't good at pretty speeches, but her next words came from an unexpected place—her heart.

"We're not getting through this unless we work together. If you're on my team, I figure that means you're on my payroll, too." She lifted both arms from her sides in a gesture of openness. "I trust you not to *fraxx* up my ship because if you do, your lives are in as much danger as mine. If you need something, the ship will now provide it to you. If you want information, you can use the ship's database. As far as I'm concerned, the *Gambit* is your home for as long as you want to stay."

She wasn't sure who was the more surprised, them or her. Did she mean what she said? Yes. Absolutely. But there hadn't been any time to really think about the situation they were in. When had she decided to make them part of the crew? Or invite them to stay on the *Gambit*? She had no idea. But it felt right.

They must have thought so too because the next thing she knew, she was caught between two hard male bodies. Their scales gleamed like molten silver, and desire shone in their eyes. "You're offering us everything we've ever wanted," Fyr'enth said softly.

"So we need to know what you want in return," Kalan said.

"We can protect you," Fyr'enth said, his mouth close to her ear.

"Or pleasure you." Kalan's eyes locked with hers. She saw his need but also the uncertainty.

She opened her mouth to speak, but before she could figure out what to say, Kalan's mouth crashed down on hers.

A firestorm of need consumed her in seconds, burning away every rational thought.

Instead of pushing him away, she reached up to tangle her fingers in his hair, using it as leverage to pull him closer. His next growl buzzed against her lips, and she answered with a low, throaty moan.

Fyr'enth pressed a hot, open-mouthed kiss to the side of her neck. She drowned in a sea of sensation. The rough touch of their beards against her skin, their hard bodies crowding hers, the low, primal growls and groans that filled the surrounding air.

Kalan's tongue tangled with hers in an erotic dance that made her head spin.

It took far too long to find the brain cells and

willpower to protest. "Stop," she finally managed to whisper. "We need to stop."

They both pulled back an instant later, and she had to fight the urge to chase after another kiss.

"Thank you."

Kalan was still so close his breath fanned her face. "For what? Kissing you?"

"Or stopping?" Fyr'enth asked.

She noticed they had a habit of finishing each other's sentences. It was too soon to know if it was going to be an endearing quirk or an annoyance.

"Both," she said and then realized she needed to tell them something. "But in the future, remember to ask permission before doing something like that. I know consent is a new concept for you both, but it's important. Touching someone without their permission is disrespectful. Plus, it can get you into a mess of trouble."

She smiled to lessen the sting of her words. "But since we're all under the thrall of this blasted mating fever, allowances should be made. I shouldn't have touched you either."

Feeling slightly abashed, she belatedly released Kalan's hair and lowered her arm.

"Consent," Fyr'enth spoke the word slowly. "I see. I give you my consent to touch me any time you like, Hezza."

"Me too," Kalan agreed.

"That's not exactly how it works but close enough." She gestured to Kalan. "Time to take a step back, Kal. Proximity to each other makes this more intense, and I think we could all use a time-out."

She caught their confused expressions and winced. "Right. Your language database won't include many colloquialisms and slang. I'll try to remember that. I'm saying that we need some time apart. A lot has happened, and there's been no time to process any of it."

"The more time we spend together, the more it affects us?" Fyr'enth asked.

"As far as I understand it? Yes. I'll tell the ship to dial up the air scrubbers to maximum. That should help for now. There's more I need to tell you about all this, but first I have to make sure I know what the hell I'm talking about. You're welcome to read up on it, too. Or anything you're curious about. If you need more information, we'll put in a request for it the next time we're in port."

They both nodded, and she got the sense they wanted to hurry to their rooms so they could start learning. It was a good time to step away.

"I'll leave you to it. If you need anything, ask the ship. If you want to talk to me, just tell the AI to connect us."

She walked away and headed toward her own quarters, which were only a few short steps from the cockpit. She had work to do, but first she needed to pull herself together.

"Ship, what's the current temperature in the freezer section?" she asked.

"The temperature in that compartment is currently minus eighteen degrees Celsius."

Perfect. Hezza made haste to the nearest ladder to the lower levels. Why waste time with a cold shower when she had a better option? She'd simply walk into the bracing air of the freezer and stay there until she could think straight. "Hey, ship, send an extra-large serving of *ja'kreesh* to that area. Will you?"

"Request confirmed. However, I must remind you that consumption of that much stimulant is not recommended. Do you wish to proceed despite this information?"

"Yes, I wish to *fraxxing* proceed," she muttered and then raised her voice to be sure the system heard her. "Do it."

"Confirmed." The ship's flat reply held an almost imperceptible hint of reproach.

Wonderful, now she was being judged by a machine. Or, she admitted to herself, maybe she was projecting. As hot as that kiss had been, she still didn't feel right about it.

Her cyborg companions didn't need a mate. They needed a mentor. Someone who could guide them as they learned to navigate their new lives. Could she do it? Yes. But they deserved more than a gray-haired cynic with a long track record of questionable decisions.

She slid down the ladder to the next deck, her hands and feet on the rails instead of the rungs. Was it the safest way to navigate the ship? No, but it was fun... and yet more proof the two cyborgs deserved someone better.

In a fit of pique, she raised one fist and glared up at the ceiling. "I've heard that the Vardarians believe they find their mates with the help of their ancestors. If any of you can hear me, I've got a message for you. You *fraxxed* up. Badly. If there's any way to undo this *sharhal* thing, do it. Let them have a chance to discover who they are before they're mated for life. They deserve to enjoy their freedom. And then, when they're ready, maybe you could find them a pretty young thing who isn't as old and jaded as me."

Once she put her feelings into words, she felt a bit better. Would it change anything? Probably not. The universe had never listened to her before, so why start now?

CHAPTER 8

KALAN LINGERED in the passageway to watch as the feisty human female walked away from them. He wanted to chase her down, push her up against the nearest flat surface, and show her just how deeply the *sharhal* was affecting him.

He was supposed to be stronger than any ordinary being, so how the *fraxx* could she walk away so easily?

"She's tougher than she looks," he sent to Fyr'enth. He could have spoken out loud, but he wasn't sure how good Hezza's hearing was.

"She is," Fyr'enth agreed aloud. "And if you go after her right now, you might find out just how tough she is. She asked for space. We need to give it to her."

"I know," he grumbled. "And I heard what she said about consent, too. Adjusting to freedom will be more difficult than I imagined."

"Agreed. But one thing I am looking forward to is falling asleep without having to listen to you snore."

Fyr'enth turned and walked into his cabin, the door closing before Kalan could think of a scathing reply.

He flipped two fingers toward Fyr'enth's cabin and then retreated to his own. Once the door closed, he slowly assessed his new home. Just the idea of having such a thing was strange. His home. His bed. His... anything.

Hezza had said the room wasn't fancy, but to him, it was a palace. The ship itself wasn't much different from Orio Station with chipped and faded paint of some nondescript color, metal grates underfoot and overhead. That's what he'd expected the cabin to be like, but he was wrong.

The interior walls were painted a warm yellow that softened the light and made the space feel warmer. Instead of metal grates, the floor was covered with a thin but nice-looking carpet. The bed was designed to extend out from one wall and took up most of the available space. That explained Hezza's earlier request to arrange the cabins to accommodate a Torski-sized passenger. This bed could handle a being that big. He eyed it carefully for several seconds. It could also fit two cyborgs and a certain human female if needed.

A quick examination determined that one wall was covered by retractable panels. Inside the space were shelves and cubbies for personal items. Not that he had any of those. A small doorway led to a sanitation room, complete with its own shower.

"Have you tried the bed? It's so comfortable I might sleep for days," Fyr'enth said through their link.

"Not yet. I'm checking out the shower. How hot do you think the water gets?"

"Ask the ship."

"Right." Having access to an AI was yet another thing they'd have to get used to.

"Ship, what's the temperature limit on the shower? And how much water am I allowed to use?"

The answer came back immediately. "You may use any temperature you wish, so long as it will not cause physical damage. As per standing orders, there are currently no limits on the amount of potable water available for use. At current staffing levels, this ship can recycle water faster than the inhabitants can use it."

He clapped his hands together in celebration. Unlimited hot water and a comfortable bed. Things were looking up.

He wanted to take a long, exceedingly hot shower, but he needed to address one thing first.

"Hey, ship? How do I arrange for new clothing? I never want to wear the stuff I'm currently wearing again."

"If you would stand in the middle of the room with your feet apart and arms out at your sides, I will scan you. Once I have your measurements, I can produce new garments."

He did as the machine instructed. Nothing happened, but the AI eventually spoke again. "Scan complete. Anomaly noted in the dorsal area that will cause challenges should you require clothing for your upper torso."

"Those aren't anomalies. They're my wings."

The AI made a series of soft clicks as if processing that information. "Information added to your file. I have no clothing patterns saved that can accommodate this feature. Would you like me to attempt to create one?"

He waved a hand in dismissal. "Not right now. I'm used to going shirtless."

The only time he'd worn anything on his upper body was when they were in EVA suits, and those had been specially made with extra space in the back to allow room for their wings. True Vardarians had wings made of membrane that folded tightly against their backs. From what Kalan understood, the first cyborg attempts had used the standard wing design, but because of the cyborgs' larger, heavier frames, flight was impossible.

One of the techs had taken pleasure in telling him in graphic detail about the terrible damage those first test subjects had endured as they attempted to modify their wing structure. Stress fractures, dislocations, and tears in the membrane had been common.

Eventually, their creators had abandoned genetics and created the cybernetic version he and Fyr'enth had.

He moved around the room as he considered clothing options. After never wearing anything but nondescript gray, he wanted something different. In the end, he gave the AI a list of items, including several that weren't clothing-related.

What he wore wasn't the only thing that needed to change.

As satisfying as it would be to set his former clothes on fire and toss the ashes out an airlock, Kalan settled for tossing them into a corner for the bots to take to recycling.

It took him a few seconds to figure out how the shower worked. The one he was used to had two settings: on and off. This one had temperature control, water pressure adjustments, and even different settings on the shower head. By the time he had it set to his liking, steam filled the smaller room. The moment he stepped under the cascade of water, he discovered what bliss felt like.

Hot water sluiced over his head and shoulders as he opened his wings and let it flow down his spine.

Several wall-mounted dispensers sat above the taps. Two were cleansers, each with a different scent. He tried the one labeled as lavender, took one sniff, and immediately rinsed off his hand. He may not have known exactly what lavender was, but he didn't want to smell like it.

The other cleanser claimed to smell like a sea breeze. Since he'd never been to a planet, he had no idea if that was true, but the scent was appealing enough.

He lathered up and scrubbed away every trace of his time as a prisoner. The hot water soothed him, relaxing muscles he hadn't known were tight.

He worked down his body, relishing every moment of this new luxury. When his fingers brushed his cock, it hardened instantly. The *sharhal's* effect might be lessened now he was away from Hezza, but it was still present.

Now seemed like a good time to take the edge off.

He fisted his cock in one hand, the slickness of the suds enhancing the sensation. He conjured up memories of kissing Hezza. The sweet heat of her mouth. The way her soft body had molded itself to his. Her breathy moans had been like music to his ears.

He moved his hand faster as he let the memories morph into a fantasy, one where he hadn't let her walk away. In his mind, he stripped her naked while Fyr'enth held her. He imagined her resisting but only at first. Her protests could be ended with well-timed kisses.

He'd fuck her with his fingers, his mouth, and then finally his cock. Yes, up against the bulkhead with her legs wrapped around his hips.

A groan rose in his throat, and he braced his free hand against the wall. Hot water flowed over him, and he pretended it was Hezza's hands caressing him, coaxing him toward climax as he fucked her.

He wanted to feel her come around him, to hear her cries as she shuddered in ecstasy around his cock.

He groaned as his balls tightened and his shaft pulsed between his fingers.

He came hard, his hips pumping frantically as his semen splashed against the tiled walls.

Fraxx. If that was what happened when he imagined sex with their lovely rescuer, what would it be like when he fucked her for real?

He couldn't wait to find out.

CHAPTER 9

Hezza couldn't be sure whether her time in the freezer had actually cooled her raging libido, or if it was simply the fact she'd kept her distance from her new guests for the last two hours. Possibly it had to do with the fact that she had the air scrubbers maxed out in hopes they could remove or at least reduce the level of pheromones on board. Or, she considered, it might be the foolish amount of Torski rocket fuel she'd consumed. She'd downed enough *ja'kreesh* that she should be vibrating right now.

Whatever the reason, her mind had cleared, and her hormones had leveled off enough to let her function. She'd spent the time mulling over star charts, calculating her fuel consumption, and trying to decide the best place to go.

After two hours, she stopped. While she still hadn't made her final decision, she'd narrowed it down to a handful of options. Now she wanted to take it to the others. This felt like a choice the three of them should make together.

She dropped the ship back to normal space and altered course enough to annoy anyone who might be following them. It wasn't a big change, and it moved them in parallel to the general direction of two of her preferred destinations without giving anything away.

It frustrated her that she couldn't tell if they were being followed. It was possible that someone had managed to detect their entry point before their energy signature dissipated. The only way to be certain would be to stay put and wait to see if another ship showed up in the next few hours. That would let her know if anyone was after them. It would also mean they'd be spotted, and the chase would begin again.

Given the choice between pessimism and hope, she opted for the former. It was always better to expect the worst. That way, anything else was a pleasant surprise.

With the task done, she rose from her chair and absently patted her stomach. She needed food, and the cyborgs probably did, too. Not that she had any idea what they'd like. From the stories Thrash and some of the others had told her about their time as prisoners of the Shadows, it was likely her guests had never had anything but nutri-bars and algae broth.

She refused to have that crap on board the *Gambit*, not even as cargo. She could still remember the way the greenish sludge would *gloop* out of the food dispenser at the corporate-funded orphanage where she'd grown up. It only came in two varieties: a watery broth that tasted like tears and old socks, or a viscous, foul-tasting gel that quivered when she poked it with her spoon.

Hezza had many failings, but no one on the *Gambit* had ever complained about her cooking. It was time to show her guests what they'd been missing.

She decided to make them one of her favorite meals. Brinner, also known as breakfast for dinner, was a tradition she started when Anya was a little girl. Whenever there was time, she'd let her daughter pick out a new recipe. Then they learned how to make it together. The food dispenser was a convenient way to get hot, nutritious meals in a hurry, but once she'd struck out on her own, Hezza discovered she enjoyed the act of preparing and cooking her meals.

Given the amount of food she expected her guests to consume, she tasked the dispenser with the job of making the pancakes. The rest she managed herself.

When she was close to ready, she sent a message over the ship's comms. "I thought the two of you might be hungry. You're welcome to join me in the galley if you want food or company."

"Thank you. We'll be there shortly," one of them replied.

She couldn't tell which, since their voices were as identical as the rest of them. At least, physically. Like most cloned cyborgs she'd met on Haven, the pair did have subtle differences. Not so much in appearance but in personality. Kalan was more forward, while Fyr'enth was the quieter of the two. She would be able to tell them apart, eventually.

Footsteps in the passageway announced that at least

one of her guests had arrived. She checked the bacon one last time and then turned to greet them...and nearly dropped the spatula she held.

Holy hells and gravity wells, a god was standing in her galley.

"Hi. Also, wow. You look different." She winced at her awkwardness, but her brain had shut down and left her to babble like an idiot.

The scruffy prisoner dressed in rags was gone. In his place was a male who looked like a leading man from the latest action vids. His long hair had been cut short at the sides, while the top had been left long enough to be swept back from his face. He still had a full beard, but now it was neatly trimmed.

He wore black pants that made her think of a military uniform—not the pretty ones they wore on parade but actual combat gear. Same with his boots. She hadn't known the ship's fabricator could even make that kind of thing. Maybe Archer had sent some new patterns along with the raw materials?

Only one thing about him hadn't changed. He still wasn't wearing a shirt.

She stared longer than she should have, too shocked by the transformation to tear her eyes away.

"Do I pass inspection?" He deliberately flexed the muscles in his arm as he casually ran a hand through his newly trimmed hair.

She blushed. Actually, *fraxxing* blushed like a teenage girl.

She huffed a laugh and waved the spatula in his direction. "You already know the answer to that."

She couldn't be certain, but something about his smile made her think this was Fyr'enth.

"Did you have any problems getting the AI to provide everything you needed, Fyr?"

It was his turn to be surprised. His steel-blue eyes widened, and he stared at her in disbelief for several seconds before finally regaining his composure. "How did you know it was me?"

"The way you smiled. You do it a little differently than your brother. One side of your mouth turns up a little higher than the other. Kalan's smile is wider. Like he's either going to burst out laughing or go for your jugular."

Fyr'enth snorted. "True enough."

Now that her brain was more or less functional, she had more questions. "Would you like me to arrange for some Vardarian-style clothing patterns? They have plenty of clothing made to fit around their wings."

He glanced down at himself as if he'd forgotten he was only half dressed. Of course, that was by her standards. To him, he was kitted out normally. "I'd be interested in trying them, if only to avoid drawing too much attention any time we're off the ship. Something to cover the wings completely might be useful, too. For the same reasons."

"That's a good point, though honestly, I think you and Kalan are going to draw attention no matter what. Vardarians aren't a common sight in this part of the galaxy." She raised a hand before he could correct her. "I know you don't see yourselves as members of that species, and I understand why. That isn't going to change the fact that everyone else who sees you is going to see two big, handsome guys with silver scales and assume you are Vardarian."

"Handsome?" Fyr'enth grinned. "Thank you."

"There's no point in denying the obvious. You were attractive before, but now?" She managed not to blush too much as she gestured at him. "You look damned good. That's not what matters, though. How do you feel?"

He took a moment to consider before answering. "I feel like myself. I'm not sure what that means yet, but this..." He touched his newly trimmed beard and then his hair. "This feels right."

"That's all that really matters," she said.

"I never liked having long hair. They used to trim it for us sometimes. Or let us have scissors so we could do it ourselves. That stopped months ago." He rolled his eyes in a very human gesture she assumed he'd learned from his captors. "Kalan stabbed one of them with the scissors, and that was the end of that."

She didn't miss a beat. "Did they deserve it?"

Her question earned her a warm smile. "They did."

Behind her, the bacon hissed and popped, reminding her she needed to check on it before it burned. Ruining this part of their breakfast would be a culinary crime. Unlike most of her supplies, the bacon came from Haven and was prepared by a skilled butcher who smoked the protein the old-fashioned way.

"Hold on a second. I need to check on this." She turned toward the pan full of fried deliciousness and started shifting the contents around.

"What is that?" Fyr'enth asked as he moved in

behind her. "It smells...I have no words for how good that smells, and I speak every language known to this part of the galaxy."

He pressed in close enough she could feel the heat of his body against her back but didn't quite make physical contact. It didn't matter, though, because his mere presence made her skin tingle and her heart race like she'd sprinted the length of the ship and back again.

"This is bacon." She forced herself to focus on her words and not the hot-as-a-star male standing right behind her.

Then she used the spatula to point to the other pans on the stovetop. "Those are scrambled eggs, and these are called hash browns. I have no idea why. They're neither hashed nor brown. They're actually seasoned cubes of potato, which makes them a vegetable, which makes this whole meal healthy."

He hummed in amusement. "I'm not an expert, but I don't think that's how it works."

She turned her head to smile back at him. "I'm the chef, so if I say it's healthy, you should nod and agree with me. Speaking of food, have you ever eaten anything other than nutri-bars and algae broth?"

He made a disgusted noise in the back of his throat. "No. But how did you know that?"

"I spent enough time with the cyborgs living in Haven to hear some stories about how they were treated while they were prisoners. I think it's safe to assume they and you have had similar experiences."

He didn't respond to her statement, but she hadn't

expected him to. Fyr'enth was the sort to take in information and mull it over before speaking.

"Is there anything else you'd like to try, Fyr? I'm happy to make anything I have in stock. I went with this meal because it's one of my favorites."

"You've shortened both of our names now. Is this a human thing?"

She laughed before answering. "It's a me thing. I tend to assign nicknames to beings. You'll probably end up with a few more before I'm done. Do you mind? I can call you Fyr'enth if you prefer. I know that's the name you chose for yourself."

"I don't mind at all." He moved in closer but still not quite touching. "I like it. Fyr. It sounds like the Galactic Standard word for fear."

She decided the bacon was done and moved the pan off the heat. "It does. Is that something you want? For others to fear you? For that matter, what does your name mean? Fyr'enth sounds Vardarian, but I've only learned the basics."

"There is no direct translation in your language. I think the closest meaning would be something like 'the oncoming storm.'"

She turned her head to look at him, only to realize he was so close her mouth brushed his for a second. She pulled away so fast she almost lost her balance. "Whoa. I didn't realize you were that close."

The smile he gave her was pure wickedness. "Must be the smell of the bacon drawing me in."

"Must be. So, Stormy, why the ominous choice of names?"

"Stormy? Another nickname already?"

"Yup, which means I'll need to figure out another one for Kalan, too."

"I can make a few suggestions."

"Did someone say my name?" Kalan walked into the galley as if he owned it. "And what in the name of gravity smells so good?"

"That is called bacon," Fyr'enth informed him.

"And it's one of my favorites...holy hells. You too?" Hezza's mouth continued talking despite the fact her brain had short-circuited again. Kalan had also had a makeover moment, and he looked *good*.

Unlike his brother, he'd kept his hair long and now wore it tied back into a sleek ponytail. His beard was little more than a thin line of dark stubble along his jaw and around his mouth. Where Fyr'enth had opted for practicality, Kalan's choices were stylish. His soft leather boots came to his knees, and his charcoal gray pants hugged his muscular thighs.

She wanted to say something about his new appearance, but then she caught the way the two males looked at each other. They had taken their first steps toward becoming individuals. She kept her mouth shut and let them have this moment.

CHAPTER 10

Kalan had walked into the galley feeling like a new male. He'd chosen everything about his appearance, from the boots on his feet to the flavor of the dental foam he'd used to clean his teeth.

His euphoria changed the moment he saw Fyr'enth. His brother, his clone, had made changes, too, and they weren't the same ones he'd made.

He cast around for the right words, but nothing suited the moment. Instead, he went with something mundane and hoped his brother understood. "Nice boots."

Fyr'enth grinned. "Same to you. I've got to ask, though. How do you expect to fight in those pants? One kick and you're going to split the seams."

"They stretch." Kalan did a deep squat to demonstrate.

"And there will be no fighting," Hezza said, her voice firm. "Even if we're being chased, they won't catch up with us until we drop into normal space and stay there for a while. Also, no friendly sparring matches until I figure out a safe space for you to do it. If you two start throwing kicks and punches, my poor ship will be the one to suffer. She's got enough dents on the outside. I don't need to add more to her interior."

"We could set up something in the same cargo bay you thought we could use for stretching our wings," Fyr'enth suggested.

"That could work," Hezza agreed. "But if you break anything, you'll be the ones repairing it. Right after I teach you how."

She pointed to the battered metal table. "There are stools stashed in a cubby on the far wall. Those will work better than chairs, since they won't interfere with your wings. Go ahead and pull them out while I get this food sorted. It won't take long."

They moved in sync, and it was oddly reassuring to see that not everything had changed.

He switched their conversation to their internal link *"You cut your hair. I didn't expect that."*

"I wanted something different. I didn't think you'd cut most of your beard off. This is strange."

Kalan nodded. *"But not in a bad way. Though I do find it odd that we chose different styles. We're clones. Shouldn't we want the same things?"*

"Apparently not. But we already knew we weren't identical in every way. This is just the first time we've been free to choose for ourselves."

They also hadn't told each other what they were doing. Each of them had done this of their own volition. All the times he'd imagined what life might look like after they'd escaped, he'd never considered that his choices wouldn't be the same as Fyr'enth's.

Kalan abandoned that line of thought for now. He wasn't in the mood for deep thoughts or hard conversations. *"I chose well. I'm not sure about your choices. The boots are good, but the hair?"* He rocked one hand from side to side. *"We should ask Hezza which of us looks better now."*

"Winner gets more bacon?" Fyr'enth asked out loud as he handed over one of the stools from the cubby.

"Deal."

"Winner of what?" Hezza asked.

They turned to find her setting a large platter laden with flat discs of something golden and fluffy on the table.

"We want you to decide which of us did the better job with our new looks," Kalan said.

"And then I want to know what those are," Fyr'enth pointed to the platter.

Hezza ignored the part about her judging them and focused on the food. "Those are pancakes. You eat them with melted butter, syrup, or fruit preserves. I usually add all three and let them fight it out for dominance, but you can experiment. Sit down, I'll bring the rest of the meal over." She smiled. "And no, there will be no contest for whose makeover came out best. You both look incredible. In fact, I want to know how you came up with the looks you chose."

"I asked the AI to show me current styles popular with males of all species. I liked this one. The bot that delivered my clothes stayed to assist me with the haircutting process with the AI's guidance."

Kalan snorted with surprise. "You let a machine cut your hair?"

"I allowed the AI to do it, yes." Fyr'enth glowered at him. "How else could I manage to do the back?"

"And that is why I bought an upgrade for the AI years ago. It cuts my hair, too. Even in the back where it's hard to reach." Hezza returned to the table with two more large plates stacked with food.

"If one of you could get the knives and forks, that would be helpful. They're in the top drawer next to the space where you found the stools."

"I'll get them," Kalan offered. "And I will help with the food. You do not have to do everything yourself, Hezza. You're paying us as members of the crew. Let us do something to earn that."

He rose and went to the drawer she'd indicated. Inside were a variety of utensils. Some he recognized, but others were a complete mystery. He'd have to ask about those another time.

"These are metal," he said as he retrieved the knives and forks she'd asked for. The knives all had rounded blades that were too dull to do much damage, but he could still stab someone with one. The forks were possibly more dangerous still.

"They are. Cheap to make, easy to clean, and they don't wear out." Hezza's eyes widened. "And I bet you weren't allowed access to anything that could be used as a weapon."

"You would be right," he said. Returning to the table, he handed a set of utensils to Fyr'enth before placing another set in a small, empty space where he assumed Hezza would sit.

Fyr'enth put his cutlery down and went back to his job of taking whatever Hezza handed him and finding a place for it on the quickly filling table.

"Do either of you know what coffee is?" Hezza asked once the plates of food were all laid out.

"I've heard about it on vids and in books, but they never gave us anything other than water," Kalan said.

"Hmm. Then maybe we'll leave that for another time. Take a seat, Fyr. I'll grab us a couple of types of fruit juice so you can try them. If you don't like any of them, there's always water."

"So many choices," Kalan murmured as he watched Hezza program her requests into the machine she called a food dispenser. He planned to ask her how to use it soon. He'd seen it making the stack of pancakes and now their drinks, so he assumed it could provide them with other items. He intended to try them all.

When Hezza was finally in her seat, they all tucked into a feast the likes of which he'd never imagined.

"This is glorious," Fyr'enth declared around a mouthful of bacon.

"If I had known that real food was this good, I'd have tried harder to escape."

"Did you do that?" Hezza asked in a gentle voice. "Escape, I mean."

It felt strange to be able to talk openly about this. "Honestly? No. In the beginning, we didn't have the will to try. Later, it was obvious we'd never make it off the station. Even if we'd reached the hangar bays, neither of us knows how to pilot a ship, and the AIs on board would not have obeyed us since we weren't crew."

"But we thought about it a lot. At least I did. We were closely monitored, so it wasn't something we could talk about, but thinking of ways to get away was how I made it through the long nights and the worst of the experiments."

"I did too. Inside our minds was the only safe place we had."

"Wait, they monitored your internal comms, too? I didn't know they could do that," Hezza said.

"They did. I couldn't even tell Kalan I'd chosen a name for myself for months. I had to whisper it to him one time when we were doing combat trials."

"I'm so sorry. You deserved so much better than to exist as nothing more than a number, even to each other."

They lapsed into silence for a few minutes.

Surprisingly, Fyr'enth talked first. "Speaking of names. You've given us both at least one nickname now. I think we should have one for you, too."

Hezza chuckled. "Actually, Hezza *is* a nickname. No one uses my legal name. Not even me."

"No one? How is that possible?" Kalan asked.

Hezza flicked out the fingers of one hand as if casting something away. "Easy. No one knows what it is. I always introduce myself as Hezza B. and then tell 'em the B stands for bitch."

"You insult yourself?" Fyr'enth asked in obvious confusion. Kalan felt the same way. Why do that?

"I like to think of it as a warning that it isn't smart to

mess with me. It works too. Most of the time." She speared another hash brown from her plate and ate it.

Kalan waited until she'd finished chewing to ask his next question. "What is your name?"

She sat quietly for several seconds as if considering her answer, or maybe deciding if she would answer at all. She put her fork down and lifted her gaze to his. "My parents named me Alyssa. My family name is Bratt. Not that I ever knew my family or my parents."

Kalan held her gaze and waited for her to continue. She knew more about them than they did about her, and he wanted that to change.

With a soft sigh, Hezza picked up the story. "I was born in an illegal colony, on a planet no one was supposed to be on. It was owned by a corporation called Dynamex. By happenstance, that's the same corporation that owned Liberty before it was forced to give it to the Vardarians for their new colony."

She flashed him a small smile. "Small galaxy, huh?"

"Why didn't you know your parents?" Fyr'enth asked.

"Because they died before I was old enough to have any real memory of them." Hezza kept her expression neutral and her voice level. If he were a normal being, that might have been enough to fool him. But Kalan was a cyborg, and he saw through her act. Talking about her past caused her pain. Every micro-expression and element of her body language screamed it, but she told them anyway.

"Have you ever heard the expression that there are two sides to every story?"

They both shook their heads.

"It's an old saying that means everyone always has their own version of events. That's because those of us without enhancements have to rely on our organic memories, which are unreliable at best. In this case, there are two very different stories about what happened to my parents, and every other adult living in the colony where I was born. According to Dynamex, there was a cascade failure in the colony's environmental controls. Toxins in the water supply, air quality issues, stuff like that. No one knows for sure because Dynamex just happened to be the ones who heard the colony's distress call. By the time they arrived, most of the population was dead or dying. The only survivors were the kids. The adults put us all into the safest building and gave us all the untainted food and water."

She tapped her chest and sighed. "I was maybe a year old at the time. I don't remember much, except being in a cramped room with other kids. We were scared. Some of us were crying. Someone came. There was shouting. That's all I remember."

Kalan found himself reaching across the table to take her hand. It was not something he'd ever done before, but it felt like the right thing to do.

She squeezed his fingers tightly. "This all happened a long time ago, and like I said, I don't remember much. I have a few fragments of memories from my life before that. A man I think was my father holding me high in the air. A woman singing while she rocked me to sleep. That's it." She looked at him and then at Fyr'enth. "I know that's more than either of you ever had. You woke up floating in a maturation pod and climbed out to discover you were prisoners. I cannot imagine what that was like."

"It was unpleasant," Kalan said. "But we survived, and so did you."

"Now, tell us the other side of the story," Fyr'enth said. Then he belatedly added, "Please."

"Since when do you say please to anyone?" He couldn't resist taking a shot at his brother's sudden act of politeness.

"You're one to talk. You're still holding her hand," Fyr'enth shot back.

Hezza—No. Alyssa—eyed them both for a beat before continuing as if she hadn't caught them talking to each other. He didn't know how she could know, but she did.

"As I said, I was too young to remember much, but there were a few older children. One of them was sent to the same orphanage as me. They remember things differently. There was no environmental failure. His parents told him that bad people were coming to make them leave, and they were going to resist. They brought him to the colony's creche and told him to stay there until they came back for him."

He squeezed her hand again in silent support, and she squeezed back. The simple but intimate gesture filled him with a deep need to protect and care for this female.

"That's the story I believe. I think Dynamex found out about the colony and told them to leave. They were stupid enough to try and fight back. My parents and every other adult there died because they thought they could take on a *fraxxing* corporation. My parents were idiots. They should have left. Instead, they got themselves killed, and I was shipped off to an orphanage sponsored by the same assholes who made me an orphan."

"Dynamex paid for your upbringing?" Kalan asked. "Why would they do that?"

"Because to them, we weren't children. We were seized property and a source of future income. Once I was old enough, they sent me for aptitude testing so they could figure out what job I'd be best suited for. That's what happened to every kid. They tested us and assigned us jobs. Since we worked for the company that sponsored us, they held back most of our pay in order to pay off the debts we incurred while growing up. They call it sponsoring, but it's really just a loan. We had to pay it all back."

"And what if you didn't?" Kalan asked. To him, this sounded like another kind of prison sentence.

"We're tagged." She pulled her hand from his so she could roll up the sleeve of her shirt. She showed them a small scar on the underside of her forearm. "Anyone who tried to leave their assigned area was identified, tracked down, and punished." She smoothed the fabric back over her arm. "I was one of the lucky ones. I showed an aptitude for piloting, so they sent me for training. I had to pay for that, too, but there are other ways to make money when your job is *fraxporting* freight from place to place. I made enough to pay off my debts before I turned thirty-five. After that, everything I earned was my own." She patted the table. "Including the *Gambit*."

"That's why you became a smuggler," Fyr'enth said. "It was the only way to pay everything off quickly."

"It was. I did it for another reason, too. If something happened to me before I paid everything off, my daughter would have inherited my debts."

Despite everything he knew about corporations, that revelation surprised him. "What? How?"

"That's the way it works. I might have bent a few laws here and there, but those assholes are the real criminals."

"They are," he agreed.

"But that still leaves me with one question," Fyr'enth said.

"What's that?" Hezza asked.

"Why do you call yourself Hezza?"

The female seated across from them grinned broadly. "When I was young, I had a lisp and couldn't say my name properly. Over time, I started calling myself Hezza instead, and the name stuck."

"Alyssa," Kalan spoke her name slowly, letting it roll off his tongue. "I like it. You can keep calling me Kal if I can call you Alyssa."

"Same for me," Fyr'enth chimed in.

Hezza pretended to look thoughtful, but he already knew what her answer would be. She liked nicknames, but he wondered if anyone had ever given her one before.

"Alright. But I'm still working on another one for you, Kal. After all, Stormy here already has two."

He blinked at her and then turned to stare at his brother. "Stormy?"

"I told her what my name meant." Fyr'enth lifted his wings in a shrug. "I don't think it struck the note of fear I was hoping for."

Kalan's only response was to laugh long and hard.

When he was finished, Hezza fixed him with a stare that could have made a charging *gharhstu* find somewhere else to be. "So, Kal. What does your name mean?"

Fraxx. Something told him she wasn't going to be impressed with his name's meaning, either.

"The executioner," he said.

Sure enough, her lips twitched as she tried to suppress a grin. "I see that subtlety isn't something either of you is familiar with. I can respect that... Cutie."

"Cutie?" He nearly choked on the word.

"Sure. Executioner. Cution. Cutie. I like it." Hezza got to her feet and picked up her plate. "Cutie and Stormy, would you please help me with my least favorite part of any meal?"

"Of course," he said, still trying to understand her logic.

"Wonderful. In that case, watch and learn the fine art of loading up the dishwasher." She pointed to what looked like a cabinet door. "A glorious invention, right up there with bacon and faster-than-light engines."

He turned on his stool and recorded everything she said and did for future reference. Which was a good thing because he didn't pay attention to a word she said. All he did was watch her move and wonder when he'd get another chance to kiss this amazing female who had scars and experiences that mirrored his own.

She was nothing like the females he'd imagined finding if they ever got free, and more than he'd ever dreamed of.

CHAPTER 11

She couldn't remember the last time her ship had been this full of life and laughter.

Her guests—no, she corrected herself—her *crew* were surprisingly good company despite the suffering they'd endured. She shared funny anecdotes about her life and even told them about how Phylomenia had recruited her onto this mission.

"Do you think they're all right?" Fyr'enth asked. "What are the chances that Colonel Barrios realized they were the source of the signal that scrambled their sensors?"

"They'll be fine," Hezza assured them. She had the same concerns, but Scott Archer was certain the device was untraceable. Even if they searched the *Bat Out of Hell* 2, they weren't likely to find anything. The source of the signal was aboard the original *Bat*, which was tucked into a hangar and was unlikely to be noticed. Phylomenia's husbands were almost as cunning as the woman herself.

"I hope so. I don't want anyone getting into trouble for helping us escape." Kalan fixed her with a meaningful look as he spoke.

It felt good to know someone was worried about her. Well, other than Anya. Her daughter's concern was a constant that had been with her for decades.

She tapped her fingers on the table as she reviewed the ideas she'd come up with earlier. Getting her thoughts in order was harder than it should have been. With an inward sigh, she realized the problem. The three of them had been together in the small galley for more than an hour, and it was apparent that in the battle between the pheromones and the air scrubbers, the scrubbers were losing.

She pulled her legs in closer to her side of the table so they weren't touching either male and proceeded. "For now, I think our best bet is to disappear. It's not a long-term solution, but it will give our allies time to react to everything that happened today. My primary focus is to keep the two of you away from anyone I don't trust, and right now that list includes most of the damned galaxy."

"Are you saying you want to protect us, Alyssa?" Fyr'enth sounded both surprised and pleased.

"Damn right I do!" She cut herself off before she said anything else. What she wanted to say would sound ridiculous. They weren't hers. "Mine" was something Vardarian males growled to their mates. Not the other way around.

"We feel the same way about you," Kalan said. He took her hand again, and this time Fyr'enth mirrored the gesture.

Uh-oh.

The connection immediately amplified the effects of the *sharhal.* Her heart rate spiked, and heat pooled low in her stomach as every thought evaporated in the blaze of lust that threatened to consume her.

"We should, uh, table this discussion until tomorrow." She tried, and failed, to tug her hands free from theirs. "It's been a long day for everyone."

"We're not tired. We're cyborgs. Remember?" Kalan's voice was more rumbling growl than real words, but she understood him well enough. His interest was obvious, and damn if she didn't like the way he looked at her. She'd had lovers. Plenty of them over the years, but this was...this was the *sharhal.*

"This is—" She tried to protest, but her brain refused to give her the words she needed.

Fyr'enth tightened his grip on her hand. "This is not something any of us expected. But does that make it wrong?"

Fraxx. It seemed unfair that he could still make rational arguments while her brain had turned to mush. It would be so easy to give in to desire and deal with the consequences later, but would that be fair to them?

"You deserve better," she blurted out the thought that had haunted her since the moment she'd felt the first stirrings of desire.

Fyr'enth shook his head. "I don't believe that. You risked everything to help us escape. Since coming on board, you've offered us food, clothing, and comforts we've only dreamed of. You even made us part of your crew."

She waved his arguments away. "I did what I thought was right. That doesn't mean I'm the female you deserve. I'm older than you and far too cynical. You two are at the beginning of a grand adventure. You shouldn't be stuck with someone like me."

Kalan bared his teeth at her. "Stop. You told us earlier that consent is important. That means we should make this choice ourselves. You can only decide what *you* want."

She didn't understand how they could be so logical about this. She also knew they were right. She couldn't make this choice for them, even if it still felt like they were getting the raw end of the deal.

"You're not wrong. I can tell you all the reasons this is not a good idea, but in the end, it's your call." She chuckled softly. "And I'd be a liar if I pretended I don't want this to happen. This *fraxxing sharhal* is no joke."

"It's all-consuming," Fyr'enth agreed.

"Is that a yes?" Kalan asked.

She stood on the precipice for one long moment, aware that once she made this leap, there would be no turning back. Then again, that ship had left orbit the moment the three of them met. The *sharhal* was irreversible and undeniable. The few who tried to resist had suffered both physically and mentally. Some had even gone insane.

"Yes. Stars help me. My answer is yes."

Kalan got to his feet while still holding her hand. "Then I think we have talked enough. We still have plans to make and information to share, but for now, there are more important things for us to do."

Fyr'enth stood up, and the two of them seemed to fill the entire galley. "Yes, there are. The first thing on my list is to claim a kiss from our mahaya." He shot his companion an annoyed look. "Because you've already had one."

"Oh no. There will be no keeping score in this... whatever this is. That way leads only to jealousy and arguments. I'd rather avoid those navigational hazards, thank you."

"I'm still claiming my kiss." Fyr'enth moved around the table and drew her off her seat and into his arms. "Then I will stop counting."

She rose and let him pull her closer, anticipation making her blood sing in her veins.

"You are beautiful," Fyr'enth murmured as he wrapped one strong arm around her waist and pulled her in tightly against his body.

She stopped herself from arguing that she was no such thing. Beautiful women didn't have white hair and wrinkles. She had both, and that was okay. The lines on her face had been carved by a lifetime of tears, laughter, and challenges. Her hair had been blazing red once, but now it was mostly white with only a few traces of flame left to remind of her youth.

No, she told herself. No doubts. No second-guessing. Not right now. It was time to let go and enjoy herself. Later, they would have to deal with the long list of challenges and potential crises. *Later*.

She rose on her toes, her hands splayed across his bare chest as she reached up to kiss him. He bent his head, meeting her halfway. His lips were soft against hers, but nothing was gentle in the way he claimed her mouth, his tongue sliding along the seam of her lips as his beard rasped against her skin.

She reached up, her fingers sliding along the hard planes of his chest to his shoulder and then higher. He shuddered and groaned against her mouth as she caressed the short hairs at the nape of his neck.

She parted her lips, allowing him entry. A moment later his tongue was tangled with hers.

This was what she needed. What she *craved*. He cradled the back of her head in one large hand, holding her in place as he took the kiss even deeper.

He pivoted to the right and took her with him. She barely noticed the move until Kalan claimed her newly exposed back. Caught between their bodies, she felt like the filling in a sinful sandwich.

When Kalan kissed the side of her neck, a wave of fire engulfed her. She moaned and tipped her head further to one side without breaking her kiss with Fyr'enth.

Both of them ground their cocks against her, letting her feel how aroused they were. Their hands were everywhere, stroking and teasing her until the heat between them ignited like a match tossed in rocket fuel.

"I don't like what you're wearing." Fyr'enth broke their kiss to frown at her. "There are too many layers."

"Ship suits were never intended to be worn in situations like this. They're comfortable and practical, but they don't come off easily."

"That's where you're wrong," Kalan nipped her ear lobe before moving away from her.

"What are you doing?" she asked, still woozy from their attentions.

"Removing an annoying barrier to progress," Fyr'enth said and then kissed her again, cutting off any chance of protest.

She almost didn't notice the sound of a drawer slamming shut. *What was Kalan up to?*

The answer came less than a minute later, when the distinctive sound of tearing fabric caught her attention. A gentle tug was all she felt followed by cool air hitting her skin.

"Much better," Kalan said, and then she saw the knife in his hand. He'd cut her clothes off!

"That's your solution?" she asked, amused and somewhat incredulous.

"It was quick, straightforward, and allowed me to do this." Kalan reclaimed his place behind her before tugging off her now ruined outfit.

She gave in to the inevitable and let go of Fyr'enth to slide her arms out of the sleeves. Naked to the waist, she wondered how long before they cut her free of the rest.

"I think you should go shirtless, like we do. It would be much simpler." Fyr'enth cupped her breasts in his hands. His eyes gleamed with desire as he growled low in his throat. The possessive, primal sound made her want to swoon.

"Show me," Kalan demanded. Hands landed on her hips, their grip firm as he spun her around to face him.

"Alyssa," he said her name like a prayer, raw and full of wonder. He dropped his head and kissed her hard enough she saw stars as sparks of desire danced across her skin.

She closed her eyes to savor the moment, and when she opened them again, she found Kalan staring down at her, his eyes burning with need. His scales had tightened until his skin shimmered like molten silver, transforming him into a work of living art.

"You are beautiful," she told him as she ran her hands along his powerful shoulders and down his arms.

"Show me the rest," Kalan said, his tone almost a command.

"Not here," she said. "My room. There's more space."

"And softer surfaces," Fyr'enth said.

"Agreed." She tried to step away from them, but Kalan held her in place.

"We know the way," he said and then surprised her by lifting her into his arms.

She laughed and threw her arms around his neck. "We should probably stop by your cabins on the way. We're going to need a bigger bed."

Of all the upgrades and improvements she'd made to the *Gambit* in her time, the one thing she'd never expected to change was the size of her single bed.

CHAPTER 12

SHE ENDED up walking the last stretch to her cabin, but there was a good reason for it. Both her males were carrying their mattresses and an assortment of bedding. She had their pillows, and the three of them formed an odd sort of parade as they made their way to her room.

"Ship, open my cabin door and retract my bed, please."

"Requested changes in progress," the AI said.

"Too bad the AI can't carry this mattress. This thing keeps bending in strange places," Kalan muttered.

"They do that. I've been assured it's just physics and they're not sentient, but sometimes I wonder," Hezza joked.

"If anything on this ship is sentient other than the three of us, I'm tossing it out the nearest airlock," Fyr'enth said.

"After stabbing it repeatedly," Kalan agreed.

She laughed and led them into her cabin. It wasn't a large room by any measure, but it was far bigger than the cabins she'd assigned to them. Most of the space was storage with a decently sized closet and cubbies for clothes, shoes, and other belongings. Unlike the crew cabins, she had room for a small desk and a comfortable chair. It wasn't much, but it gave her a place to deal with the paperwork that was a surprisingly large part of the job.

Her soon-to-be lovers set the mattresses down beside each other. They covered nearly half the room and stretched from wall-to-wall. That done, they laid out the blankets they'd brought while she tossed the pillows in a heap on one side.

Good enough.

They must have felt the same way because the second the bed was made, they started to undress. She joined them. Was it sexy? Not really, though she did enjoy the view. Silver scales, hard muscle, and... damn. Everything she'd heard about Vardarian anatomy was true.

If her intel about their size was accurate, could her other tidbit of information be right, too?

Without saying anything, she walked up to Kalan and gently ran her fingers up his spine. As she reached the spot between his wings, he sucked in a breath and shivered.

Oh yeah, it *was* true.

"What did she do?" Fyr'enth asked sharply.

"I don't know." Kalan spun to face her. "Do that again," he demanded.

Feeling brazen, she moved in close enough that his cock was pressed to the soft curve of her stomach. Then she reached around to stroke the sensitive spot between his wings.

He groaned and shuddered as he rocked his hips against her. "That is...how did you know to do that?"

"It's something I heard about on Haven."

"Show me," Fyr'enth said.

"Wait your turn," Kalan snarled and snaked a possessive arm around her waist.

She ignored his outburst and gestured with her free hand. "Come stand beside Kal. I'll show you."

As Fyr'enth moved into place, she looked up at Kalan. "Being together means sharing everything, even our pleasure."

Fyr'enth clasped his brother on the shoulder. "She is *ours.*"

Kalan kissed her gently before speaking again. "Yes, she is. Our *zana.*"

"What does that mean?" she asked.

"Treasure," Fyr'enth said, his voice soft.

Something shifted deep inside her, like a missing piece of her life suddenly clicked into place. Choked with emotions she couldn't name, she reached up to stroke Fyr'enth's back. She wasn't ready to deal with feelings right now. Tonight was about something else.

Pleasure.

When they moved, it wasn't in the direction she expected. Instead of the makeshift bed, they led her to the chair near her desk. It was larger than was practical for the space, but she liked it too much to get rid of it. It was well-padded, with an upholstered back and a wide seat framed by solid armrests. She'd even fitted it with magnets that ensured it stayed put no matter how wildly she maneuvered.

"The chair?" she asked. "Why not the bed?"

"We have something in mind, and the chair works," Fyr'enth said.

They guided her into the position they wanted, and she willingly complied with their instructions. Soon, she kneeled on the seat with her arms crossed over the back of the chair. Her knees sank into the cushions, and the soft fabric caressed her bare legs and belly.

"Not quite," Kalan said. He moved beside her, one hand cupping her breast. He coaxed her upward, until her breasts hung over the back of the chair with her arms braced across the top.

Only then did he move in front of her, letting her see him fully.

The only word to describe him was beautiful. He was all hard muscle and perfectly sculpted features, like a statue cast in the purest silver.

Gently, she wrapped her fingers around Kalan's cock, stroking it slowly from root to tip.

To her delight, his scales shimmered in response to her touch. She knew it was just a reflex, but it made her feel powerful to have so much of an effect on this big, dangerous male.

She stroked him again, her grip firmer this time. He groaned and reached down to take her breasts into his hands. He ran the tip of one finger around each nipple several times before rolling them between his fingers and giving them a light squeeze that made her gasp.

"You liked that?" Kalan asked.

"I did. Do it again, please."

"So polite," Fyr'enth said. "Do you think she'll ask so nicely when she begs for release?"

She turned to look over her shoulder in surprise. She'd expected Kalan to be the dirty talker of the pair. "It's always the quiet ones," she said.

His grin was pure wickedness as he smoothed both hands down her back and then over the curve of her ass.

Pleasure piled upon pleasure as they explored her body and learned what she liked. After a while, she thought of something.

"As much as I hate to say this, one of you needs to let go of me and retrieve something from the cubby near where my bed was. On the left side, near the corner."

Kalan sighed. "Now?"

"Trust me, you'll want what's in that bottle," she assured him.

He had to be guided to the right spot, but the little bottle was exactly where she remembered putting it. She'd never used it, but Saral had gifted it to her during a previous visit and had insisted she keep it, "just in case."

"What is this?" Kalan asked once he'd returned.

"*Uli* oil," she said as she opened the cap and poured some of the contents onto her upturned hand. "It's a pleasure-enhancing oil. A friend of mine on Haven gave me some." She caught his scowl and clarified. "A happily mated *female* friend."

In an effort to end the discussion, she placed her oily fingers on his cock and spread more of the oil across his skin. His next breath came out in an explosive hiss, and his cock twitched between her fingers.

"*Fraxx.* What is this friend's name? I need to thank her someday."

"Her name is Saral, and she would say no thanks are needed so long as you provide me with orgasms."

He grunted and thrust his cock into her hand.

Fyr'enth laughed. "That, we can do." He leaned over, his body covering her back as he took the bottle from her.

A moment later, a warm trickle of oil flowed across her lower back. Her skin tingled and heated as the oil worked its magic.

Kalan took it next, coating his hands before spreading it around her breasts.

The three of them quickly fell into a rhythm, and soon she was writhing between them, panting with need.

When Fyr'enth drew two of his fingers down her spine, she shivered and then tensed in anticipation as he moved further down, following the seam between her cheeks to her sex. When he parted her folds to stroke her clit, she moaned and rocked backward, her fingers still gripping Kalan's hard cock.

Their touches grew hungrier as they pushed to the peaks of pleasure.

At one point, Kalan took her hand from his cock and placed it on one of her breasts. She understood immediately and pressed her breasts together, giving him what he wanted.

He pushed his hard length into the valley between her breasts, groaning as she bowed her head so she could lick the tip of him at the apex of every thrust.

Fyr'enth toyed with her clit until she was wet and shaking with need. Only then did he slip two long fingers into her pussy. She ground herself against his hand, moaning as one fucked her pussy while the other pumped his cock between her breasts.

She almost drowned beneath the waves of pleasure that slammed into her from every side. Her orgasm came hard and fast, tearing through her like a firestorm and leaving her breathless in its wake.

It was the best sex she'd ever had, and she wanted more of it.

CHAPTER 13

FYR'ENTH WATCHED as their glorious female climaxed, her body gripping his fingers as she shuddered and gasped with pleasure. She was nothing like the females he'd been ordered to fuck on the station. They'd always been wary, even the ones who'd come back time after time.

Hezza didn't fear them. She wanted them as much as they wanted her, and that made her even more desirable. The body she'd dismissed as too old for them was beautiful. Her skin bore lines and scars that spoke of a lifetime of experiences and misadventures.

He wanted to hear the story behind every mark and memorize every part of her. She was their *zana*, a treasure beyond price.

As she came apart between them, his fangs dropped, and he had a sudden urge to sink them into the skin of her throat. His dick throbbed and twitched as the thought took hold. Yes, he wanted that. To fuck her until she came around his cock and then came again as he bit her and let her blood flow over his tongue.

He forced the idea out of his mind for now. He had more important things to focus on.

He withdrew his hand from between her legs and raised it to his mouth. The rich fragrance of the *uli* oil blended with her essence, and the scent triggered a fresh wave of need.

He had to be inside her. Soon.

He fisted his cock with his oily fingers. "Are you ready for me, *zana*?"

She turned her head and nodded. Then she parted her legs and arched her back to give him access to her body.

He moved in close, stroking himself again and again. He knew she wanted him, so he took his time, drawing out the moment before they both got exactly what they needed.

When he finally positioned himself at her entrance, she was trembling with need. Gently he eased into her, his breath exploding in a hiss as he sheathed himself in the heat of her body.

If this was the effect of the *sharhal*, he hoped it never faded. This moment blew every fantasy he'd ever had to atoms and replaced it with something so much better, and achingly, perfectly real.

He raised his head in time to see her reaching for Kalan. She caught him by the hips and pulled him close so she could take his cock into her mouth.

His brother cursed and bucked his hips as he cradled

her head in his hands. Their gazes locked, and Kalan's voice sounded inside his head. *"Ours."*

Fyr'enth didn't reply. He didn't have to. This wasn't just a moment of pleasure. It was the beginning of something that would change both of their lives.

Smiling, he leaned down to press an open-mouthed kiss to Hezza's shoulder, letting the points of his fangs glide along her skin without hurting her.

When she moaned, he began to rock his hips in slow, easy thrusts, letting himself go deeper each time. The *uli* oil added new sensations, intensifying everything. It seemed to be doing the same for Hezza because he could hear cries, even muffled as they were by Kalan's cock.

Soon, they fell into a back-and-forth rhythm. When one of them thrust into her, she'd be pushed toward the other one. The pattern held for several glorious minutes, but eventually the rhythm faltered as they all started to lose control.

He gripped her hips as he sped up his thrusts, driving deep into her channel as her inner walls gripped him tightly.

"Fraxx," Kalan groaned as his vision filled with stars. He wouldn't last much longer.

Fyr'enth grinned at him. "Bet you break before I do."

Hezza reacted before he could. Her fingers sank into the flesh on his hips as she pulled him closer. She made a low, throaty humming noise he didn't understand at first. What was she doing?

The answer became obvious when Kalan threw back his head and groaned their *mahaya's* name.

"I think she took that as a challenge."

She hummed an affirmative noise that sounded like *uhhuhmm*.

He slapped her lightly on the ass as he fucked her. That made her moan even louder, and Kalan's control snapped. He bucked his hips against her face, his motions almost frenzied and his expression wild.

"Almost..." he groaned in warning.

Every female they'd been with had always pulled away at this point but not Hezza. She hummed again and reached between Kalan's legs. Fyr'enth had no idea what she did, but the results spoke for themselves. His brother roared, his voice echoing off the walls as he came.

Fyr'enth withdrew, holding off his next thrust to give Hezza time to enjoy Kalan's response before he drove his cock home with enough force that their bodies met with an audible slap. It didn't take long for him to reach his own climax. He came hard, emptying himself inside her as he slumped over her back, covering her body with his.

Her release came mere seconds after his. She moaned, shook, and tensed as pleasure overtook her.

It took longer than he expected to gather up the shattered pieces of his mind and return to full awareness. His face was buried in Hezza's hair, allowing him to breathe in her scent. He rose slowly before reluctantly withdrawing from her body.

"When I woke up this morning, I had no idea the night would end like this," Hezza said. Her voice was breathy and low.

Kalan looked up to grin at him. "She thinks the night has ended."

He caressed her hip and grinned back at his brother. "Oh, *zana*. No, this isn't the end. This is just the beginning."

CHAPTER 14

Anyone who traveled the void knew that time moved differently there. The distance between stars was too immense with no landmarks to pass. Day and night were meaningless constructs marked by the dimming of the lights at a certain time. Crews learned quickly that the only way to avoid losing track of the days and stumbling around in a fugue was to stay busy.

Hezza was pleased that Kalan and Fyr'enth embraced this new way of life with surprising ease. She'd been worried that after a lifetime of enforced idleness and restrictions, they would struggle with the unending list of chores that filled most of their waking hours.

She ensured that they had enough downtime to watch vids and read through the ship's database of information on any topic that caught their interest, but otherwise, something was always needing their attention.

By the second day, it was clear that the ship ran better with a crew to help her manage things. By the third day, she wondered how she'd managed to do it without them.

They had the size and strength to accomplish things she couldn't have. While they didn't have the skills or knowledge needed to make the repairs themselves, they were eager to learn. She taught them everything from how to bang out dents to overhauling the hydraulics that controlled the heavy hatches, which sealed the ship in case of a breach.

As she moved through the ship, she saw the changes, and it made her smile. The *Gambit* felt alive again, and so did she. Was it the *sharhal*? In part, yes. She was riding high on endorphins, pheromones, and mind-meltingly good sex. That wasn't all of it, though. She *liked* them. They were good, decent beings with personalities that were a mix of hard edges and surprising innocence.

Did she still have doubts? Some. But it was hard to be cynical when things were going so well.

They hadn't done much talking that first night, but in the morning, they'd come up with a plan over coffee, waffles, and more bacon.

She'd explained the risks and rewards for each potential destination. They'd asked her pointed questions that made her consider things she hadn't before—like if anyone there might recognize the ship despite the fact she'd swapped transponder IDs. The *Gambit* now appeared to be the *Artful Dodger*, a cargo vessel registered to a small corporation from a backwater part of the galaxy.

Was it legal? Hell no. But it was another layer of protection. One she should have used back at Carnax

Station, but she'd been certain the IAF wouldn't be looking too hard for her.

She wouldn't make that mistake again. Not when the stakes were this high. Another error she'd made last time was trying to go it alone. While many of her friends and compatriots weren't around anymore, Phylomenia's reappearance in her life had shown her that she still had friends she could call on, as well as her daughter. She'd always taken care to keep plenty of distance between Anya and the shadier parts of her life, but this was different. Anya would want to help this time. The trick was finding a way to let them all know she needed them.

She knew someone on Taza Four who could make it happen, but she didn't know if Flek was still there or if he was still in the game. They wouldn't know until they got there, which would take days of travel.

"Ship, where are the rest of the crew right now?" If they weren't doing anything pressing, it might be a good time to introduce them to the weapons systems. She really hoped they wouldn't be in any firefights, but she wanted to be prepared for anything.

"Crewmembers Kalan and Fyr'enth are currently in cargo bay three."

Of course they were. She should have guessed as much. That was the bay she'd suggested they use as a recreation area. It was the largest open area on the ship, with enough height to allow them to stretch their wings and fly—or at least glide. She'd shown them how to adjust the gravity in that section to make it easier for them to stay airborne despite the lack of air currents.

They'd turned one corner into a makeshift gym. The

weights were all cobbled together from spare parts, but they made it work. She avoided that area, though—not because she was averse to exercise, but her cyborg lovers had decided they wanted more of a challenge and increased the gravity in that small area to twice normal.

She had enough trouble with the slightly heavier gravity when she visited Haven.

The doors were open as she approached, which let her hear the clank and slam as one of the pair lifted weights she couldn't have moved if her life depended on it.

She stopped at the doorway, one shoulder pressed into the frame, and watched. Kalan had his back to her, his wings outstretched as he squatted while holding a bar with what looked like engine parts strapped onto each end.

She knew every scar on his body now, though she hadn't heard the history behind all of them. The play of muscles beneath his scales made her hands itch with the need to touch him. The *sharhal* no longer made it impossible to think, but her libido was still running in overdrive.

Tearing her eyes from Kalan, she spotted Fyr'enth soaring the length of the bay. When he reached the far end, he banked and turned, letting him see her.

"*Zana*," he called down to her. "How long have you been watching us?"

"Hey, Stormy. I just arrived a minute or so ago."

Kalan set down the weight bar and turned to smile at her. "Hello, Alyssa."

She got a tiny thrill every time they said her name. If

anyone else dared to use it, she'd have kicked their ass into the middle of next week. But with them, her usual rules never seemed to apply.

"I thought you two might want some time working with the ship's weapon system. If you're busy, though, it can wait."

"Not busy," Kalan said quickly. "You know how much I love blowing things up."

She laughed and wagged a finger at him. "But only in simulations. Missiles are expensive!"

She made it into a joke, but the reality was that she didn't have a lot of money on hand. Flying around the galaxy doing good deeds might be fulfilling, but it also meant she hadn't completed a single contract in the last two months. She had to assume her accounts would be watched, so she couldn't access what little savings she had. That was another reason they were headed to the Taza system. She hoped someone there might buy out her contract for the goods she had on board.

As she considered their situation and how much to tell them, Fyr'enth flew over to her while Kalan made his way on foot.

Fyr'enth reached her first and drew her into his arms for a long, hot kiss that banished all her worries.

He held on to her even after the kiss ended. His gaze was locked on something behind her. She assumed it was Kalan.

"Now?" he said suddenly.

"Now," Kalan replied.

"Now what?" she demanded. She hated not knowing what was going on.

Fyr'enth sighed and brushed a gentle kiss to the tip of her nose. "I wanted to wait and do this tonight over dinner." He glared over her shoulder at his brother. "When we weren't sweaty and in need of a shower."

"We've waited long enough already," Kalan said.

Hezza placed a gentle hand on Fyr'enth's chest and stepped out of his arms so she could see Kalan.

He dropped to one knee with his hands resting on his thigh. Fyr'enth joined him, the two of them so tall they were almost eye level with her even kneeling.

"Cutie, Stormy. What's this?" she asked.

"We have something for you," Fyr'enth said.

Kalan reached out and held up one hand, uncurling his fingers to reveal a data stick. "We want you to have this."

She took the device, still unsure what was going on. "I'm missing something."

Fyr'enth nodded at the item she held. "The contents of the data stick are important but not as important as what we're doing." He scowled. "This is why I wanted to wait, Kal. We needed more time to practice."

"Practice what?"

"Explaining," Kalan said. "We've been learning about Vardarian culture. It's traditional for males to offer their *mahaya* a blade at some point during their early courtship."

Fyr'enth continued the line of thought. "The blade represents the males' intention to protect their mate."

She knew about the tradition. What she didn't understand was why they were talking about it when they had made it clear they didn't see themselves as

Vardarian. She kept her confusion to herself and waited for them to explain.

Kalan touched her hand. "We don't think you need our protection, Alyssa."

Fyr'enth placed his hand over Kalan's. "Well, maybe a little."

Warmth filled her chest, and a smile played at the corners of her mouth. "Fair enough. I have been known to attract trouble from time to time."

Kalan smiled back at her, the tips of his fangs showing. "The information on the data stick was given to us by someone on Orio Station. She said it contained everything she could gather about the research being done there and what they did to us. We want you to have it."

His hand tightened around hers. "You don't need our protection, but you have earned our trust. We trust you, Alyssa. With our lives, and with the information you hold."

Her chest tightened as a tidal wave of emotions crashed over her. She felt honored and unworthy at the same time. Blinking hard to hold back her tears, she nodded. How had they gotten here so quickly? And why did it feel so damned right?

She already knew the answer to her question. It felt right because it *was* right. All of it. Every bit of chaos and craziness had led to this moment. It wasn't just the ship that felt renewed. She felt it too. She had a fire in her soul that had been missing for a long time.

She just wasn't sure it would last.

"Thank you," she finally managed to say. "I'm not

good with feelings, but right now?" She touched her chest with her free hand. "My heart is full of them."

They rose to their feet, their metallic wings hissing slightly as the feather-like structures slid over each other.

"Have you seen everything on here already?" she asked.

Kalan nodded. "We have. It explains a great deal but doesn't tell us everything. I can say that it contains damning evidence against the ones who created us, including their names and images of their faces. We trust you to know who to send this information to. I want revenge..." He withdrew his hand and clenched it into a fist.

"But we'll settle for justice," Fyr'enth finished.

"If we have to," Kalan said, looking so disgruntled she had to laugh.

"Revenge never feels as good as you think it will," she told them once she could talk again. Then she held up the hand with the data stick. "This will change things. I know who needs to see it, and I promise, they will find a way to make them pay."

She tucked the device into a pocket. She'd have to review it all, of course, and she wasn't looking forward to that. It was necessary, though. As hard as it would be, this wasn't a scenario where she could choose ignorance. She had to know.

She toyed with the data stick as she considered what it might reveal as well as what potential problems it raised. At the top of the list was the simple fact that if the enemy figured out they had this information, someone would be sent to retrieve it.

They did not need that complication, but when did the universe care about what she wanted?

"Is there anything I should know right now?" she asked.

Kalan growled. "Yes."

"Details?" she prompted.

"The files revealed the identity of the one in charge of Orio Station," Fyr'enth answered while Kalan continued to snarl under his breath. "Her name is Detta Ani, and she is Vardarian."

Holy *fraxx*. "Vardarian? One of your own did this to you?" She held up a hand in apology. "Sorry, I know you don't think of yourselves as Vardarian. After this, who can blame you? I don't understand how someone can turn against their own this way." She raised her hand to pinch the bridge of her nose. "No, I can understand it. Greed. Someone found this bitch's price and then paid it."

Another thought popped into her head, and she looked up at them. "Wait. You didn't know about this? Didn't you see her or sense her somehow?"

"We had no idea." Kalan looked more dangerous than she'd ever seen him. "None of us did. If any of us had known, we'd have shared that information no matter what it might cost us."

"I bet," she said, still trying to wrap her head around this revelation.

Fyr'enth looked at her intently. "Do you think the Vardarians will react strongly to this news? When the cyborg project was first revealed, the humans' response seemed weak."

"You'll need to dig deeper to learn about the real outrage and pushback once the project was made public. The corporations hold too much power, and that means their version of the story is the easiest to find. There was so much of an outcry that the government had to take a stand and force the corporations to free the remaining cyborgs. Not to mention handing over unimaginable amounts of money as restitution.

"As for the Vardarians? I know the prince will be incensed. I don't know much about his sister, though. She wasn't happy her brother triggered a diaspora, and I know she doesn't really approve of Tyran being mated to a human. Nor is she thrilled that he and his *anrik* are in love with each other as well as with their *mahaya*." She shrugged. "But when she learns about this? I imagine she will shed her scales."

They both gave her startled looks. "That can happen?" Fyr'enth asked.

"What? Oh. Not really. It's an expression I learned back on Haven. At least, I don't think it actually happens."

"That's good." Fyr'enth lightly tapped his forearm. "It wouldn't be much use as armor if it could potentially fall off."

"There's too much we still don't know about our bodies," Kalan agreed and then fixed her with a hot-eyed look. "But we did find out why we've been feeling the urge to bite you, *zana*."

"I told you about that. It's part of the *sharhal*."

"You didn't tell us everything," Fyr'enth said. "We understand it better now. It's about more than simply giving each other mating marks. It's how we exchange our nanotech. Since you don't have any, that would mean you would carry ours."

"I'm not sure that's a good idea." The second the words left her mouth, she wanted to take them back. The sentiment was right, but her delivery sucked harder than a black hole.

They both glared at her. "Why not? Having nanotech would give you so many advantages," Fyr'enth said.

"And it would help protect you from harm," Kalan added. His jaw was tight, and even his wings seemed to quiver with disapproval.

"One. I thought we just agreed that I don't need your protection. Two, if we do this, there's no going back." She scrambled to try and find a way to explain her concerns without making things worse.

"It's only been a few days. We don't know if this is a forever thing."

"You've said that before, but we've read all we could. So far every match between our species has resulted in a permanent bond," Fyr'enth said.

"That's the thing, though. You've already pointed out that you are not Vardarian. Not completely. What if something happens that changes things? We could end up like some of the other species that are compatible. You've read about those?"

"We have," Kalan said.

She relaxed a little. If they'd already learned about this, they'd know it was a real concern. "Then you know that matings between your species and others happen, complete with the *sharhal,* but it doesn't always stick. Sometimes the bond fades away."

Fyr'enth spoke next. "What we have will not fade away, Alyssa. You'll see it when you review the files yourself. They tried to change us, to block that response so we'd never experience the sharhal. It didn't work. That's one of the reasons they deemed us to be failures. Killing machines are supposed to obey orders without question, and they cannot be allowed to have feelings... or find their mates."

"That's not who you are!" she protested.

"It's not," Fyr'enth agreed and moved to stand shoulder to shoulder with his clone.

"We are your *mahoyen.* You are ours, *zana.* And we are yours. Always. Why don't you believe this?"

Kalan's question pierced her heart and left her bleeding inside. Her first instinct was to argue, but she waited for one heartbeat and then another. She exhaled a breath she'd held too long and felt some of the tension leave with it.

Were they right? She let herself consider that for a moment and found herself smiling. Yeah, they were. This was happening. Then she stopped and reworded that thought. This *had* happened. She was mated to these two breathtaking males.

"I do believe it." She took a deep breath. "I'm your *mahaya.*"

For one sweet, perfect moment she was suffused with joy. But of course it didn't last, because reality reared its ugly head and intruded with yet another issue.

They both moved toward her at the same moment,

but she threw a hand up to stop them. "But that still leaves us with a problem to solve."

"Why are you still finding reasons to deny this?" Kalan demanded, his tone sharp.

"I'm not. But this is…" she waved her hands as she tried to find the right words. "I believe we are fated to be together. That's not the issue. The nanotech is a problem, though. I don't know anyone my age with that kind of upgrade. I'm not young. What will it do to me? How long will I live once I have it? Will I get all the benefits or just some of them because parts of me will be too old or worn out to repair? We don't know. I'm sure someone at the colony does, but we can't talk to them right now."

Kalan still looked grumpy, but he didn't interject.

"You want to wait until we know more?" Fyr'enth asked.

"I do. Hells, we don't even know what kind of nanotech you're carrying. Is it a Vardarian or a human design? Was there any mention of that in the files you gave me?"

They both went still and their eyes unfocused, which she'd learned meant they were accessing their onboard databanks.

"There's no mention of it," Fyr'enth confirmed.

"Does it matter?" Kalan asked.

"I think it does." Hezza organized her thoughts for a second before explaining further. "There are differences, though not as many as there were at first. From what I understand, Vardarian tech has a sort of countdown clock that lets them live a long time but not forever. They age, but it's a slow process without a lot of the aches and illnesses that beings like me have to deal with."

She smiled ruefully. "In case I haven't mentioned this yet, aging sucks."

"But if you took the nanotech, you'd be free of all that," Kalan said.

"Maybe. There's no way to be sure until we talk to beings who know a lot more about this stuff. And that's just the Vardarian tech. For the human cyborgs, it's different. No one knows how long they'll live. Some theorize they could go on for centuries, maybe even longer. They're working on changing that, but I don't know how far they've gotten."

She took their hands in hers and squeezed. "I want to have a long life with you both. I really do. But before I make this decision, I need more information."

Fyr'enth sighed. "I would still prefer it if you had the healing and abilities the nanotech would provide, but I understand."

Kalan pulled his hand away. "I don't."

"Kal," she said his name softly.

He shook his head. "I understand that this is another consent thing. I cannot force you to do this, but I don't like it."

He turned and stalked toward the door.

"Where are you going?" she called after him, even knowing she should just let him go. He needed time. So did she.

"I need a shower."

Well, at least he answered her.

Fyr'enth raised her hand to his lips and kissed her fingers softly. "I'll talk to him. This has all been..."

She finished the sentence for him. "A lot. I know. You go. I've got reading to do."

After Fyr'enth left, she stayed in the cargo bay. The place felt empty now, and to a small degree, so did she. Unsettled, she set off for her quarters. For the first time since meeting her mates, she felt alone.

It wasn't a good feeling. Hopefully it wouldn't last long.

Hopefully.

CHAPTER 15

Sleep eluded Kalan all night, and he wasn't happy about it. The only thing that helped his mood was the knowledge that no one else on the *Gambit* had slept any better than he had. He knew that because his enhanced hearing let him hear Hezza's soft exclamations and curses as she read through the contents of the data stick they'd given her.

She'd let Fyr'enth know she wanted privacy to review the files, and he'd relayed the information to him.

Did it sting that she didn't tell him directly? Yes, but he also knew that was self-inflicted pain. She was giving him space because that's what he needed.

He still didn't like it.

Since she was staying in her cabin, their nightly routine had gone out the airlock. Instead of preparing and sharing the evening meal, she'd sent a request to the food dispenser through the ship's AI, and then had one of the bots deliver it to her door.

She'd taught them how to use the dispenser, so it

wasn't like they'd go hungry, but the food hadn't tasted as good. They'd eaten in silence, cleaned up, and gone back to their own cabins.

He hadn't liked that, either.

Since coming aboard, they'd spent every night on the makeshift bed in Hezza's cabin. Last night was the first time he'd gone to bed alone. He'd lasted an hour before getting up and opening his cabin door.

Fyr'enth's was already open, which told him that his brother was having the same issue. They weren't used to being alone. In the beginning, several pairs of cyborgs had been in their cell block. Over time, that number had decreased, but even at the end, the two of them had shared a cell.

Worse, he didn't have Hezza within reach. He couldn't believe how quickly he'd adjusted to her presence. Not just in in his bed but in his life. She could soothe his nightmares with a touch or a softly murmured word, and her smile banished even his darkest thoughts to the back of his mind, at least for a while.

Without her, his mind drifted, conjuring memories of his former life. Recollections of forgotten pain. The faces of the other research subjects. Did they have names, too? He'd never know, because most of them were gone. Every time one of them was taken, he'd wonder if this would be the last time he saw them. When the one they took was Fyr'enth, the fear would twist his guts into knots.

They'd always sent the same message to each other at those moments. "Be strong."

Even that had been a risk, but it was better than saying nothing.

A few hours before the ship switched over to daytime mode, Fyr'enth asked, *"Do you miss her, too?"*

"Yeah."

He could actually sense his clone's annoyance through their link. *"Then fix it."*

"Got any idea how? It's not like we got uploads on relationships."

"No fraxxing clue. But maybe when we get to Haven, we can ask if they have something like that."

"Understanding your mate, made simple," Kalan joked.

"For you? They'd have to make it really simple. Small words and lots of pictures."

"Fraxx *you*." He flipped off his brother, not caring that he couldn't see the gesture.

After that, he settled down a little. Enough to shake off the grasping hands of the past and start untangling the feelings tripping him up in the present.

By the time the lights in the corridor came on, he still had a lot to think about, but now he knew where to start.

Breakfast.

"Hey, ship, what breakfast foods does Hezza make the most?" he asked. The AI wouldn't understand if he asked it what her favorite foods were, but it could tell him which ones she made often.

"Do you wish for me to include the previous four days in my data set? There has been a marked increase in the consumption of such foods since she added you to the crew roster."

"Good point. Leave the last few days out. She was cooking for us, not for herself."

"Here is the list of foods. I have ranked them with the most commonly requested at the top."

A list appeared on a screen affixed to the bulkhead in front of him. Bacon. Eggs, with a notation that scrambled was the most common variation requested. Toast was next on the list, and the last item was baked beans.

He read the last line again. *Beans?* Time to clarify things with the AI. "Are you sure about that last one? Alyssa, I mean, Hezza, claims she's not a fan of vegetables in general."

"My data is correct. Baked beans is a dish made with legumes slow cooked in a tomato-based sauce."

Okay, that made more sense. Actually, it sounded delicious. "Since she hadn't made those yet, he'd surprise her with some. He'd heard her claim several times that the food dispenser always messed up the bacon, but he knew how she liked it. Crispy but not crunchy with a bit of give. How hard could it be to do that himself? The food dispenser could handle the rest.

It took him a while to get the food dispenser programmed for everything, and he had to override the portion sizes to make sure there was enough for everyone. A single loaf of bread wouldn't make that much toast. Would it? His language database gave him several definitions of what a loaf was, but none of them sounded that large.

"Ship, where does she keep the bacon?" he asked once the food dispenser had started on the meal.

"In the refrigeration unit. Lower left shelf," the AI replied. "Do you wish for me to increase ventilation in the galley?"

"Lower left, got it. Why would you increase the airflow?"

The ship's AI made a soft humming sound but didn't reply. If he didn't know better, he'd swear it didn't want to answer his question.

"Ship?" he prompted.

"On more than one occasion, members of the crew who have attempted to cook have created situations that produced large amounts of airborne particulates. Specifically carbonized foodstuffs."

"You mean they burned their food."

"Correct."

"I'm not going to burn the bacon." Hezza would not be happy if he ruined one of her favorite meals.

The AI didn't respond, so he continued his prep. He retrieved the bacon and the same frying pan he'd seen her using the first time she'd cooked for them. He set the pan down on the stovetop, and then poked at the controls until a red light came on as a round section of the surface started to heat up.

It took him several minutes to separate enough bacon from the main block. By then the pan seemed relatively hot, so he dropped a handful of the meat strips inside.

The meat hissed and sizzled a surprising amount, but it settled down fairly quickly. While it cooked, he went looking for the tool Hezza had used to move the bacon around when she cooked. A spathel? Sapucla? He checked his language files. Ah. A spatula. An odd name for something so simple.

He found what he was looking for in a cupboard and turned back to the bacon.

The sizzling had started again, this time accompanied by a popping noise. He hurried back to the stove and poked at the slices.

The meat hissed at him like an angry animal and hot gobs of fat spattered everywhere. Some landed on his bare chest.

"Ow!" he yelped and swiped at the affected scales.

Annoyed, he prodded the bacon again. Hezza hadn't had this issue.

This time, some of it stuck to the pan, so he tried to pry it loose with the spatula-thing.

The result was more hissing, more spitting, and more burns. Worse, the pan was starting to smoke a little. He would *not* admit the AI was right about his cooking skills and ask it to activate the ventilation in the galley. No. He could deal with this.

He spread his wings slightly, using them to fan the air and hopefully dispel the smoke.

The bacon wasn't forming the neat, crisp strips they had when Hezza cooked. Instead, they were clumped together. The ends looked almost done, but the middle was still raw.

Fraxx.

"Need a hand, Cutie?" An amused female voice came from somewhere behind him.

"You're ruining my surprise." He turned his head to smile at Hezza. Instead of her usual ship suit, she'd chosen to wear a pair of soft, gray pants that hugged her legs and hips. Her top was dark red and sleeveless with only a pair of thin straps that crossed over her shoulders. Her slicked-back hair was damp from a shower, but she didn't look refreshed. Her eyes were puffy, and the lines on her face were more pronounced.

"And, yes, I think I need some help."

She joined him at the stovetop. When she held out her hand, he gave her the spatula but stayed where he was. He wanted to see what she did to fix this mess.

"The trick with bacon is to lay each strip separately from the start. It also helps if you do it before the pan gets too hot." She pointed to the controls. "You have the setting too high."

She changed something on the controls, and the red light turned amber. Then she used a fork and the spatula to pull the strips apart. He'd added too many to fit into the pan the way she did it, so she set some of it aside to cook once the first batch was done.

He expected to feel embarrassed or defensive about his screw-up, but he didn't. The moment she had appeared, he began to feel better. Had he *fraxxed* up breakfast? Yes. But it was easier to move past than he'd expected. Unlike the ones who'd created him and forever tried to push him past his limits, she didn't have expectations. She simply accepted him.

It was a new feeling, and he liked it.

The food dispenser dropped two more slices of buttered toast onto a surprisingly full plate.

Hezza nodded toward the machine. "How much toast did you ask for?"

"I'm not sure. How much toast is in a loaf?"

She laughed, and the sound wrapped around his soul like a caress. "More than we can eat. Looks like we're having bacon sandwiches for lunch today."

"Sounds good to me."

"Me too. I'll have to see if we've got any fresh tomatoes left. The *Bright Arrow* had a hydroponics bay full of fresh vegetables. I think it was mainly for the officers' meals, but I managed to get my hands on some."

"The same way you acquired the upgrades to the *Gambit*?" he asked.

"Pretty much. A little banter, a little bribery. The usual."

"I want to learn how to do that." His words surprised them both.

She hesitated before answering. "It's what I'm good at, so yeah, I can teach you if you want, Kal. With so many paths to choose from, are you sure you want to follow mine?"

His first reaction was frustration, but he didn't lash out. He made himself stay calm and repeated her question in his head. Anger had made him walk away yesterday. It hadn't solved anything then, and it wouldn't now. He needed to do better.

After a long silence, he did his best to explain the churn of emotions he felt. "I'm not sure of much right now. I don't even know what questions to ask to learn what I need to know." He placed a hand on her hip and turned her to face him. "What I do know is this. I trust Fyr'enth with my life." He leaned in close and whispered so his lips brushed hers. "And I trust you with my heart. Wherever your path leads, I will be at your side, *zana*."

Her cheeks darkened with a rush of blood. Before he could ask what that meant, she kissed him. The soft, sweet kiss was somehow more enticing than any other moment they'd shared.

Kalan cupped her face in his hands, and their mouths mated, their gazes locked. The emotions in her eyes mirrored everything he felt—doubt, frustration, attraction, and something else. A tenderness that made his heart ache.

"I want this," he murmured against her lips. "I want you."

"I want this, too." She smiled, her eyes brightening. "All of it. Even the biting and the nanotech. This isn't about you and Fyr. I've learned some hard lessons in my life. One of them being it's safer not to want too much. That way, you won't be disappointed." Her hand covered his. "I need a little more time. Will you give it to me?"

He understood her better now. She wasn't doubting him or the mating bond. She doubted herself. He knew that feeling well.

He leaned down to kiss her gently. "I would give you anything. Take the time you need." Then he dropped his voice to a growl. "I never want to sleep alone again."

"I don't want that either." She turned her head toward the food dispenser. "Which reminds me. I came in here to get a fresh mug of *ja'kreesh*. I didn't sleep last night, and it's going to be a long day."

"No more *ja'kreesh* for you. It's not good for someone your size." He flashed his fangs. "At least, not until you accept our nanotech. Then you can have as much as you want. Though you won't need it. Think of all the things we can do with the time once you don't need so much sleep."

Hezza pursed her lips. "That's true." Then she snickered and patted his cheek. "You know, I don't think you're going to need much instruction on how to talk other beings into giving you what you want. You're already *fraxxing* good at it."

"I'm a fast learner."

"Yes, you are. Because they were wrong about you and Fyr. You're not failures at all. You're survivors."

A hiss from the frying pan reminded them that the bacon was still at risk of burning. They moved apart with Hezza tending to the cooking while he changed the settings on the food dispenser to stop it making any more toast. While he was at it, he reduced the amount of everything else he'd programmed in.

Once things were nearly done, they plated everything and put it on the table.

"Do you need some ointment on those burns?" Hezza asked.

"No. They're already healing, and I reduced my ability to feel pain until they stopped stinging."

"Handy skill," she said, but her eyes were still on his bare chest. "So, you don't need me to kiss them better?"

"Does that work?" Not that he cared either way. He wasn't turning down any opportunity to have Hezza kiss him.

"Does it actually help you heal? No. But it does help distract the patient." She smiled, her green eyes twinkling. "Just in case they start to sting again."

"Better safe than sorry," he agreed.

"Then we should call Fyr and tell him it's safe to

come out of his cabin. He's probably bored and hungry by now."

"He'll survive," Kalan wasn't ready to share her with his brother yet.

"True. But then breakfast will get cold. It's been a very long time since someone cooked for me. I'd like to enjoy the experience."

That he could agree to, especially since he was the one who'd done the cooking. "Then we'll eat soon. What's on the agenda for the rest of the day? More lessons on ship maintenance?"

Hezza shook her head. "Not today. I think we've all earned a day of rest." She lowered her voice to a sultry whisper and laid one hand on his chest. "Or at least, a day in bed."

He wrapped his arms around her and drew her in until her head was tucked under his chin. She nestled against him, her cheek pressed to his chest.

"That sounds perfect."

CHAPTER 16

Hezza wasn't sure she believed in the afterlife. If such a thing existed, the last few days with Kalan and Fyr'enth had to come close. They'd laughed, hugged, fucked, and even danced together a time or two. Could it last? Of course not. Knowing that made every moment sweeter and every memory more precious.

Today's morning meal had passed in near silence because they all knew things were about to change. They were about to drop back to normal space as they entered the Taza system and made their way to a colonized moon orbiting Taza Four.

While the system was far from the main trade routes, the existence of the agricultural colony combined with the mining outfits on the planet itself brought enough traffic to make it a small but significant trade stop.

They'd come here in part because she hoped someone would buy her current contract and finish her deliveries. The other reason they were here was to see an old friend and ask for a favor. If he was still here.

Now that they were about to enter the system, it was time to find out.

"Ship, how long until we drop into normal space?"

"Transition will occur in ninety-seven seconds."

"Good. And the recorded messages I made are buffered and waiting to be sent?"

"Affirmative."

She felt a bit silly for even asking the question. The AI wouldn't deviate from her orders unless she told it to. "Sorry for doubting you."

The apology made her feel even sillier. There was no need to apologize. The AI was software. She hadn't even given it a personality upgrade, for *fraxx* sake.

"Your apology is unnecessary but appreciated. I have detected an elevated heart rate and body temperature. Do you have concerns I should be aware of?"

She laughed. "I'm worried about a lot of things right now, but it's all messy, organic being stuff. You just keep us flying straight and true, and I'll take care of the rest."

"Understood."

"You two ready to set foot on an actual planet? Well, a moon, but close enough."

Fyr'enth sat in his newly modified seat, which was now more of a stool with a vertical bar where the safety harness was attached. "More than ready. Do you think we'll get a chance to fly?"

She'd already thought about this. "It's not like we can hide your wings, so you're going to attract attention no matter what. Even if someone makes a report, we'll be long gone before the IAF or anyone else can get here. Don't do it until we're clear of the port, though. No sense in annoying the local air traffic control center. They'll get tetchy and probably try to fine me for operating *unregistered aircraft* in their airspace."

"We are not aircraft," Fyr'enth sounded insulted.

"Doesn't matter to them. They'll find something with a nice juicy fine attached and try to make it stick. We'll know it's bullshit, they'll know it's bullshit, but that won't change anything."

"We are now entering normal space," the ship's AI announced, ending conversation on the topic.

Stars filled their viewscreens. Some of them weren't stars at all but planets too distant to appear as more than balls of light.

"Which one are we headed for?" Kalan asked. As usual, he was behind them in the gunner's seat.

"We're headed for a moon orbiting this planet." Hezza pointed to the largest monitor and then tapped on the screen to zoom in until one planet filled most of the screen. It was a nondescript place, colored mostly gray and brown.

"That is Taza Four. It's rich in ores and minerals but short of almost everything else. Minimal water, a slightly toxic atmosphere, and not a lot of anything other than rocks. The only populations are in the mining camps and processing stations."

She tapped the screen again, and they got their first view of the moon that was their true destination. From this distance, it wasn't much more than a green and blue sphere.

"There's a colony on that moon. The original goal was to be able to grow enough food to support themselves and the miners on Taza Four. It's gone so well that now they have a surplus to sell or trade with other colonies."

"The corporation that owns this system is okay with them trading the goods away?" Fyr'enth asked.

"There's no corporation out here. We're in Pheran territory, and they've signed over the rights to the system to a cooperative. The corporations aren't thrilled about it, but they can't dictate to the Pheran government the same way they can with humans."

"We've only ever met one Pheran. The one that gave us that data stick." Fyr'enth scowled. "I worry about what happened to her."

"So do I. I got the feeling she wasn't a willing participant in the project," Kalan said.

"Once we land, you're going to see Pherans, humans, and even a few Torskis. Hell, the last time I was here, a handful of Jeskyrans were trying to set up shop. Flek was not happy about that. I imagine he's run them off by now. But in case they're still around."

She turned to look at them both. "If you see orange and yellow beings with lots of thorny protrusions and wearing nothing but a loincloth? Do not make eye contact. If they try to sell you something, say no and walk away. If they try to give you anything? Do not take it."

"Noted," Fyr'enth said.

"Who is Flek?" Kalan asked.

"Flek is the exception to everything I just said. He's a friend and the only decent member of his species I have ever met. He's the contact I told you about."

"Your contact is a member of one of the most untrustworthy species in the known galaxy?" Fyr'enth gave her a sidelong look that held more than a hint of confusion.

"He is. His day job is running a local pizza shop. But his real source of income comes from buying and selling information. If anyone can get the information on that data stick to the ones who need to see it, it's Flek. Just don't stare at him too much."

"He'll take offense?" Fyr'enth asked.

"Hell no. He won't care, but Jeskyrans are not an attractive race by any measure. If you look too long, you might lose your appetite, and his pizza is delicious. Trust me, you don't want to miss out because you didn't listen to me."

Several seconds passed in silence, and then Kalan grunted. "I would like to unsee that," he muttered.

She cackled as she realized they must have checked their onboard databanks for information on the Jeskyrans. "I warned you!"

"You did," Fyr'enth agreed. "But that was..."

"And most of them have personalities to match their appearance. Like I said, Flek is the exception to the rule."

The conversation faded after that, which suited her fine. She was trying to calculate if they'd need to buy another fuel cell while they were here while sending messages to traffic control to let them know about their arrival.

They were less than an hour away when she received the message she'd been waiting for. Flek's diner was still open for business, and he'd reserved a table for them at the requested time. He also confirmed that he still served his special dessert and was happy to make her a batch.

That last bit had a double meaning. It told her Flek would take the job and move the information she had. It also meant that she'd be coming back to the ship with an order of freshly baked cinnamon and sugar dusted bits of leftover pizza dough.

It was good news all around, and she happily shared it with her *mahoyen*.

They were still peppering her with questions about the night's meal when they finally entered the moon's atmosphere.

Unlike the planet it orbited, the moon had water, plants, and a breathable atmosphere. The gravity was lighter than standard, but the colonists had adapted by adding gravity plates to most of the building interiors.

She placed them on a course that would take them to the colony but would also allow her passengers a chance to get a good look at a view she always enjoyed.

"I think you'll want to see this," she said as a range of mountains filled the viewscreens.

The peaks were impossibly high, rising to jagged points marked by lines of perfectly white snow. In some places, the wind had blasted the snow away, revealing ridges of blue and gray stone.

"That is beautiful," Fyr'enth said, his eyes locked on the screen in front of him.

"Imagine flying over that," Kalan said. His voice held a note of longing she'd never heard before.

Clouds dotted the sky, some of them clinging to the peaks as the planes flew overhead. Where they blocked the sun, they left shadows that dappled the snow.

After a few minutes, a river appeared. It snaked

through the valley below the mountains. In some places it was a brilliant turquoise while in others the sun's reflection made it shine like silver.

Over time, the blue peaks softened, becoming rolling hills covered with trees, and then finally flattening out into grassland. Eventually, the green and gold grass gave way to farmland with crops of various types turning the land below into a patchwork of color.

They all watched the viewscreens, though she stole glances at the males from time to time. They never looked away, and the expressions on their faces told her everything she needed to know.

For them, this was their first real look at what freedom meant. She was so glad to share the moment with them.

She didn't speak until the colony showed up as a gray smudge on the horizon. "Welcome to Taza's lunar colony."

The buildings took shape as she pointed to the main viewscreen. "In about ten minutes, we'll be breathing unfiltered air, and you can take your first steps in real gravity. It's lighter than you're used to, so take that into account when lifting anything or pushing off the ground to fly."

The two males grinned at her and then at each other.

Whatever the future held, today they'd finally get to fly. Today would be a good day.

She hoped it wouldn't be their last.

CHAPTER 17

Fʏʀ'ᴇɴᴛʜ ʜᴀᴅ ᴅʀᴇᴀᴍᴇᴅ about this moment for as long as he'd lived. They'd experienced plenty of planets in sims, but this was different. This was real.

They walked down the gangway, every footfall clanging on the metal ramp. When his boots hit solid ground, the sound changed to a dull thud.

"We are now dirtside," Hezza said. "How does it feel?"

Fyr'enth planted his feet on the ground and raised his head to look up at the sky. A pale blue expanse filled his vision. Apart from a few scattered clouds, it was as open and inviting as he'd imagined. A cool breeze flowed around them. This wasn't an artificial air current created by a fan but a natural phenomenon.

He opened his wings slightly, letting the air push against his metallic feathers.

"It feels good. Better than that, but I don't have the words," he said.

Kalan hummed in agreement. "The sun is warm on my face. I didn't expect that."

"Sims are wonderful things, but they can't replicate everything," Hezza said.

"They didn't get the smells right, either. They tried, but the program could only create one at a time." Fyr'enth inhaled through his nose. "There are so many scents here."

He knew some of them, but others were a mystery. The biting tang of rocket fuel was familiar, as were the faint traces of someone cooking food. A warm, musty scent might be from the livestock pens they'd seen as they'd flown into the port.

While they took in their new surroundings, a slender female with dark skin and long black hair approached.

He stiffened, but Hezza calmed him with a touch to his arm. "It's fine. She's part of the ground crew."

"Welcome to Taza Four's lunar colony. I can't locate any documents listing cargo for offload or pickup. Is that correct?" The female spoke Galactic Standard, but he couldn't place her accent. Despite addressing Hezza, the female kept looking at him and Kalan.

Hezza cleared her throat. "Hello, Sajita. I'm hoping to transfer a contract and leave the cargo here for pickup by another party. If that happens, I'll file the paperwork, but there's no sense in you doing all the work if I don't have any takers."

"Oh, of course. I'll make a note of that," Sajita said, but she didn't look down at the data tablet in her hand. Instead, she let her gaze roam up and down his body.

Hezza chuckled, but there was no warmth in the

sound. "Do you want me to do your job for you? Because it looks like you're busy ogling something that doesn't belong to you," she said. Her voice remained soft, but the underlying tone was full of steel.

"I'm just appreciating the male form. If they're interested, I'd be willing to let them appreciate my form right back."

Hezza's lips curled up in a snarl. "Back off, Sajita."

The female tore her eyes away to give Hezza a haughty look. "You don't own your crew. They can make their own decisions."

"We have already made our decision." Kalan placed a possessive hand on Hezza's shoulder while Fyr'enth walked past Sajita to place his arm around her waist.

"Hezza is our *mahaya*," Fyr'enth declared.

The other female blinked in surprise, but then her expression turned sour as her eyes went cold. "What a waste. How much does she pay you? I can't imagine any other reason why two hot young males like you would spend time with a shriveled hag like her."

Hezza's next words came out with a guttural growl that would have done any Vardarian proud. "I don't have to pay them, sweetheart. They're with me because I am the only female in the whole *fraxxing* galaxy who can give them everything they want or need." She took a small step toward Sajita. "Starting with respect. Since you don't have any for yourself, I can understand why you find it difficult to give it to anyone else. Now find somewhere else to be, or I'll report you to someone so senior you've never even heard their name."

Sajita's dark skin turned ashen in the brief moment before she turned on her heel and hurried away.

"I would report her anyway. If I knew who to complain to," Hezza muttered as the female fled the area.

"But you said you'd tell one of her senior supervisors?" Kalan said.

Hezza lifted her shoulders in a shrug. "I lied. Beings like her only get away with that kind of behavior because no one is willing to call them out on it. Sure, she could make things difficult for me here, but we're not moving cargo right now, so she's got no way to threaten us."

Fyr'enth tugged her back to his side and nuzzled her cheek. "You are hotter than a supernova when you get growly and possessive, *zana*."

"Now you know how I feel when you do it," she replied, her cheeks stained with color. "But enough talking. We have places to be and beings to meet." She jerked her thumb in the direction Sajita had gone. "And something tells me she won't be willing to let us extend our stay longer than the three-hour window I set up before we landed."

She led them out of the port by following the pathway painted on the tarmac. Different colors led to different places.

"If something happens, come back here and follow the blue line back to our section of the port," she told them.

"You're expecting trouble?" Kalan asked.

"I always expect trouble, but I don't think we'll have any. With all the jumps and navigational changes we made, even if someone is chasing us, they'll be hours behind."

"Do you think you'll get a buyer for our cargo in the time we have?" Fyr'enth asked. It didn't seem likely.

"Oh, we will. Flek is already working on that for me. We haven't agreed to anything, but if there're no takers here, he'll likely buy the contract himself. He'll take a cut and sell it on to someone later."

"But you told that female there was nothing to offload," Kalan said.

"I told her what she needed to hear. I've dealt with her before, and every time I do, things go mysteriously missing, but by the time I notice, I'm light-years away and can't do anything about it. Flek will know who to trust and get them to handle the transfer."

"You lied to her," Kalan sounded more amused than concerned.

"I did." Hezza stopped walking but held on to their hands, so they both stopped and turned back to look at her. "When I told you that I bend rules and do questionable things, I meant it."

Fyr'enth shook his head. "You protect yourself and those you care about. I don't see anything wrong with that."

"Me neither," Kalan agreed.

"And this is why I've stopped questioning the universe's decision to put us together." She smiled and squeezed their hands. "We have matching kinds of crazy."

"We do," Fyr'enth agreed.

The breeze stiffened, whirling around them with

enough strength to push the debris on the ground around their feet. An idea came to him, and he seized it immediately.

"Today we've walked on real dirt and breathed unfiltered air for the first time. Now I think it's time that you experienced something new."

With that, he pulled her closer and then scooped her into his arms.

"What the *fraxx* are you doing?" she demanded. "Put me down!"

"You said we could fly once we left the port." He sent a mental image of his plan to Kalan, who whooped in response.

"I said you can fly. You two. The ones with wings!"

"You don't need wings, *zana*. You just need to hold on to me."

He tightened his grip and bent his knees as his wings unfurled behind him.

Hezza swore softly and threw her arms around his neck. "If you drop me, I'm leaving you to rot on this moon," she warned.

"I won't drop you," he promised.

And then he took to the air.

Kalan launched at the same time, the wind from their wings making the detritus and dust on the ground scatter.

They cleared the buildings in seconds and then began to circle as they rose higher into the infinite blue of the sky.

"Which way?" he called to her once they were high enough to see the entire colony.

"Now you ask me that?" Hezza lifted her head, and he realized she'd been hiding her eyes all this time.

When she saw how far up they were, she tightened her hold on his neck. "*Fraxx!* This is very different from flying a ship!"

They had to shout to be heard over the wind, but he understood her well enough, and there was no missing the note of exhilaration in her voice.

He felt it too, from the tips of his wings to the bottom of his soul. *This* was freedom. From up here he could see every part of the small colony, including a square of packed dirt near the center. Brightly colored tents were set up without any discernible pattern to the layout. Some were clumped together while others stood alone, and one group made a sort of triangle if you squinted and looked at it sideways.

Avians in cages squawked loudly in front of one tent while a vendor in an open area stood over baskets and crates full of harvested plant matter. The smell of roasted meat and other savory things made his stomach grumble. It was time to find this diner and learn why Hezza kept talking about something called pizza.

It took only a few minutes to reach the diner. From above, it looked like every other building in the area—a two-story, weathered structure with "Flek's Diner" painted on the roof in large yellow letters.

"The paint was cheap, and he wanted every pilot that flew over his place to know it was there," Hezza explained when asked.

The diner didn't look any better once they went inside. The furnishings looked battered, some of the floor tiles were cracked, and the whole place looked faded, save for a single mural on one wall that had never been finished.

"Don't worry about how it looks. The pizza is to die for, and they brew their own beer. I'm partial to their ale myself, but you're welcome to try anything that piques your interest."

"Is that you, Hezza?" someone called from behind a closed door. When it opened, Fyr'enth got his first look at a living Jeskyran. He was almost as tall as they were, but far more slender. Long thorns jutted out from his shoulders with shorter clusters distributed over the rest of his body. His skin was orange mottled with yellow, and he wore nothing but a loincloth that hung halfway to his knees.

"Hey, Flek. You're looking good." Hezza raised her hand in greeting. "Still enjoying your own cooking too much?"

The male patted his naked stomach, carefully avoiding the thorns. "You know it."

"Flek, before we get down to the serious business of pizza and beer, I want to introduce you to someone. This is Kalan and Fyr'enth." She paused and then said, "They're my *mahoyen*. My mates."

The Jeskyran beamed and threw his hands in the air. "Wonderful news! Congratulations!" As he spoke, he shook his hands and fingers rapidly. "Your drinks I buy. The pizza you buy."

Hezza raised her own hands and briefly shook them in Flek's direction. "Thank you. I'll have an ale. Since these two are new, why don't you set them up with two flights of your best?"

"We'll take a seat while you make dinner. Then we can talk."

"Yes. Yes." Flek pointed to a table in the back corner. "So you can watch the door. Yes?"

"You know me too well."

Once the owner had vanished back into the kitchen, they sat down at the table. It had a bench on one side, but two stools on the other, which meant they could all sit comfortably.

"What was..." Kalan shook his hands in imitation of Flek. "That?

"His race doesn't hug or touch each other much because of the thorns. They use their hands to express their emotions. That was his way of showing excitement and celebrating with us."

"Ah." Kalan nodded.

It did make sense. The clusters of thorns would make any kind of physical contact problematic.

Flek reappeared before they could ask any more questions. He busied himself behind the counter for several minutes before coming out with a tray with one large glass of amber liquid and two sets of smaller glasses.

"Ale for you," he set the larger glass down in front of Hezza. "And flights for you two." He placed the smaller collection of glasses down and then pointed to each glass in turn. "A honey lager. A golden ale. This is a berry stout, and this," he pointed to the last glass, which held a dark, froth-covered liquid. "This is a chocolate porter. Very good."

Then he looked at Hezza. "Your pizzas are in the oven now. We have time to talk. I made them early because you are regular. Like a clock. Not like some other customers."

He didn't sit down, but he did move closer, his eyes never leaving the door.

"You seem uneasy, friend," Hezza said.

"Strange things happen. Too many new faces. Too many questions. It may be time for me to move on." His thin lips almost vanished as he grimaced.

"You should move to The Drift. A new station is opening there. Defiance. Plenty of hungry customers." She winked. "And not just for pizza."

The Jeskyran nodded. "A friend suggested this to me before. But he said come to Astek Station." He flicked out his fingers. "But that blew up. Might happen again."

"It might. But you have to go somewhere," Hezza pointed out.

"I will think about it. Now is not the time for my problems. Tell me about yours."

Hezza explained their situation, somehow keeping most of the details to herself while still painting a clear picture of their issues.

She finished by saying, "So, I need information sent to Haven. It will need to be secure and heavily encrypted. I'll pay. It also has to get there fast. Know any couriers who could handle the job?"

Flek nodded rapidly. "Do. Do. Anything else?"

Hezza slid the data stick across the table to Flek. "I need another copy sent to a former IAF colonel named Scott Archer. His ship's the *Bat Out of Hell* 2. You remember Phyl Harrington? She married him and another fellow, Garrett Michaels. Any of them can be the recipient, but no one else."

She paused before adding, "And this is the big ask. I need a copy sent to the empress of the Vardarian Empire."

Fyr'enth's head snapped around to stare at her, but Kalan spoke first. "You what?"

She gave them both a firm look. "You heard me. She needs to know what had been done. Someone stole genetic material from her citizens. You might not see yourself as Vardarian, but what about the others? You don't get to make that choice for them."

She was right, but that didn't make him feel better about it. What if this empress tried to order them back to the empire? That wouldn't end well for anyone.

Flek watched their conversation intently. "You say these are Vardarian cyborgs? Like the corporate soldiers but not?"

"They are. Consider that information a bonus payment. Just don't pass it on for a month. That will give everyone involved time to deal with the immediate problems."

"A month. Yes. Reasonable." His eyes glittered. "But then, I make scrip selling it. Some will pay large for such information." Flek held up one hand. "But no one that would do harm to you or yours. That is not my way."

"I know. That's why I'm telling you."

After that, the conversation shifted to talk of payments and finding a contractor for the cargo on the *Gambit*. Until then, Flek was willing to pay to store it.

By the time Flek brought out the pizzas, everything was settled and Hezza had instructed the ship's AI to start offloading the cryo-pods and their mysterious contents.

Fyr'enth followed along, but most of his attention was on the feast laid out in front of him. Hot dough smothered in toppings, including a generous amount of melted cheese.

One bite was all he needed to decide that he and Kalan needed more of it in their lives. The question was, why hadn't Hezza introduced them to it already?

Was she holding out on them? Was the food dispenser not capable of creating something this complex? He would find out.

"Which of these drinks do you prefer?" Kalan asked via their internal link at one point.

"The honey lager." The light, slightly sweet taste appealed to him.

"I like the stout."

It didn't surprise him that they'd chosen different beverages. The longer they were free, the more they learned about themselves. They'd always known they were not the same in every way, but the list of differences grew as the days passed. It was strange, and sometimes he disliked the changes. He knew some things would always stay the same, though. They would always share a face, and they'd love the same female.

The thought startled him.

Love? He hadn't known the word was more than an abstract concept until recently. Even then, he hadn't expected to experience it himself. But sitting there, enjoying a meal with the only two beings he cared about, he realized it was true. He loved his brother in one way, and he loved their *zana* in another.

His revelation was cut short by a strident series of chirps from the comm device Hezza had given him before they left the ship. Kalan's and Hezza's went off at the same time.

"*Fraxx*," Hezza muttered as she fumbled in her pocket. He handed her his device, instead.

She activated the screen and cursed. "We need to go. Now! An IAF ship is entering the system. We need to be gone before they try to lock down the port."

"Try? Yes. Do?" Flek shook his head. "They are not in charge here. You go anyway. Be safe."

"No time to pay. Sorry Flek. Put it on my tab, and I'll pay you the next time we meet."

"Yes. Go now. Pay later."

They were almost to the door when he shouted, "Wait. I have your dessert ready!" He grabbed a bag from beneath the counter and tossed it to them, somehow avoiding snagging it on his thorns.

Kalan caught the bag and tucked it under his arm. *"I've got these. You take Alyssa."* He sent through their link.

"No one ever stays for dessert. Always rushing." He managed a grin that revealed far too many teeth. "You were never here. Yeah?"

"We were not," Hezza agreed.

The flight back to the *Gambit* felt like it took forever. Where was the IAF ship now? Was it already in orbit?

It was not. Adrenaline had made time crawl, but in

reality, it took them less than six minutes to return to the ship. They still had time to do...something.

"What's the plan?" Kalan asked as they strapped into their chairs in the cockpit. The ship's AI had already started the preflight process, and they were only minutes away from being able to take off.

"Message incoming. All bands and frequencies. I apologize. I am unable to block the signal," the AI announced.

It was audio only, a female voice as cold as the void they were about to return to. "Attention, citizens of Taza Four's lunar colony. This is Lieutenant Commander Heath of the Interstellar Armed Forces ship *Falcon*. Be advised that we are in pursuit of a fugitive. Anyone assisting Captain Bratt, also known as Hezza B, or the crew of the *Desperate Gambit* will be prosecuted under Galactic law. This is your only warning. Do not interfere."

"How the *fraxx* did they get here so fast?" Hezza cursed as her hands flew over the controls.

"Ship, we're leaving. Give me full manual control and prepare for evasive maneuvers the second we clear the atmosphere."

Fyr'enth glanced back at his brother. He recognized that name, but from where?

Kalan had a thoughtful look on his face, too.

"*The Bright Arrow*," they both said at the same time. That was it. The female in command of the *Falcon* had been the one they'd heard speaking to Barrios when they'd made their escape.

"You sure?" Hezza asked. "What am I saying? Of

course you're sure. You're the cyborgs. I'm just the squishy meat sack flying this ship."

Any reply was cut off when she hit the thrusters and the *Gambit* took off vertically.

"I think I've said this before," she grunted through gritted teeth as the ship fought to break free of the moon's gravity. "Brace yourselves. This next bit is going to be fun."

At least this time, he knew what her definition of the word meant. Fyr'enth grabbed his harness and braced his feet against the deck. They were on the run. Again.

CHAPTER 18

THE *FUN* DIDN'T last long. Hezza knew they were screwed before they left the planet's gravity well. The moon's orbit had it on the same side of Taza Four as the approaching IAF ship, and by happenstance, its rotation also had it facing toward the *Falcon*.

The ship chasing them was already close enough for a target lock, and no amount of fancy flying would change that.

"We need a new plan," she said before explaining the problem. Then she turned to look back at them, her stomach tied in knots and her throat thick with fear. She could not and would not lose them.

"Any suggestions?"

"That female is from the *Bright Arrow*, which means she's been after us since the beginning," Fyr'enth said.

"And despite all the course changes and tricks you pulled, we never lost them," Kalan said.

Fyr'enth finished the thought. "Which means they're tracking us."

She'd come to the same conclusion. "Someone on the *Bright Arrow* slapped a tracker on the *Gambit* while I was parked on their flight deck. Those *fraxxing* sneaky sneaks!"

"Sneaky sneaks?" Kalan chortled. "That's the best you can do?"

"I'm busy trying to think of a way out of this," she protested. "I'll come up with something better before we tell anyone this story. If we live that long."

"We're not dying today." Kalan's tone was raw and edged in defiance.

"No, we're not."

While they talked, she continued to fly them away from the incoming ship. It wasn't much of a plan, but it bought them more time to come up with something else.

After three frantic minutes of brainstorming, they had only one idea. It was horrible, dangerous, and desperate, but it was the only shot they had.

"You're sure you can do this?" she asked them for the third time.

Kalan bared his teeth in frustration at her question. "Yes. We spent hours in the sims learning now to spacewalk. Will it be the same doing it for real? No, but it will be close enough."

She'd muted the AI for this conversation. She didn't need tactical updates or another reminder that they were being hailed by the *Falcon*.

Sending the males she loved into the void in badly fitting suits that could barely accommodate their wings felt like the wrong call to make, but none of them had any choice.

"Do it." She undid her safety harness and stood up so she could face them both. "One of you will need to stay inside and manage the tether. Do not leave the *fraxxing* airlock until the ship's AI has found the tracker. No sense in risking yourselves until we know where the bastards hid it."

"We'll suit up and stand by." Fyr'enth unstrapped, stood, and pulled her into his arms for a sizzling kiss that made her wish they could just go to bed instead of dealing with this mess.

"You do that," she held him longer than she should have before slipping past him to do the same to Kalan. "And don't you dare get yourself hurt. Do you hear me? I'm tired of facing the universe on my own. If I can't do it with you at my side, I'm not doing it at all."

Kalan hugged her so hard she heard her ribs creak. "We're not going anywhere without you. Not even into whatever lies on the far side of death."

"I'm holding you to that."

When she finally let them go, she waited until they were out of sight before she allowed a few tears to fall. She hadn't felt like this since she'd first held her tiny daughter in her arms and realized that she would die before letting anything happen to her.

Anya had been the center of her universe once. She still was in some ways, despite being a grown woman with a life and mates of her own. What she felt for Kalan and Fyr'enth was different but also the same. They were her everything, and she wasn't giving them up to anyone.

She'd die first.

With that upbeat thought at the front of her mind, she sat down and buckled in. Then she got to work.

The *Falcon* was still far enough away that they shouldn't be able to intercept her communications. Especially not if she used a tight beam to relay the message directly to her intended recipient.

The downside? The receiver would be easy to identify. Or they would be, if Flek wasn't good at his other profession.

"Ship, you're off mute. Please locate one of Flek's data buoys. You have the list of codes and transponder keys in your database. I need one close enough to hit with a tight beam communication, and I need you to find it fast."

"Scanning now."

While the AI did its thing, she composed a quick letter summarizing the situation and asking Flek to grant her another favor. If he came through, she'd owe him more than she was comfortable with, but it would be worth it.

She read through it once, corrected a couple of misspelled words, and called it good enough. "Hey, ship? When you find the buoy, send the message I just encrypted and saved to memory."

"Confirmed."

"Alright. Then it's time to start the show." She took a deep breath and composed her features into what she thought of as "serious captain mode."

"Ship, is the *Falcon* still hailing us?"

"They are."

"Then open the channel. It's time Lieutenant Commander Heath and I had a chat."

The officer in charge wasted no time with pleasantries. Not even a hello. Her voice came through even before the visuals were established. "Who am I speaking with?"

Since the entire point of this conversation was to stall for time, Hezza didn't answer until saw the other woman's face on her screen. She was young for her rank, which immediately made Hezza wonder if talent had earned her the promotion or something else. The military claimed it was immune to nepotism and bribes from the corporations. She'd be more likely to believe them if they claimed the heart of every star was filled with chocolate.

"This is Captain Bratt of the *Desperate Gambit*. I don't think we met while I was traveling on the *Arrow*. What can I do for you, Lieutenant Commander?"

Heath's ice-blue eyes narrowed, and Hezza could swear she saw one eye twitch slightly. Good. A high-strung young officer looking to make a name for themselves was something she could work with.

"Captain Bratt. You are under arrest for the illegal transport of restricted alien weapons and the attempted sabotage of an Interstellar Armed Forces vessel. I am ordering you to shut down your engines and prepare to be boarded. Any resistance will be met with lethal force. Do you understand?"

Hezza had to repress the urge to laugh out loud. Was the lieutenant commander's bun so tight it had cut off blood flow to her brain? Sabotage? Alien weapons? Was that the best they could come up with on the long flight here?

"I have no idea what you're talking about. I've done nothing to any IAF vessel." That much was true. Archer was the one who'd somehow managed to convince the entire task force they were under attack.

"Are you refusing to comply?" Heath demanded.

"I'm not refusing anything. I'm just stating my innocence for the record. I assume you are recording this."

She flicked her gaze to the small screen that showed an outline of the *Gambit* and a progress bar. The scans were underway, but so far there was no sign of the *fraxxing* tracker.

Hezza held up her hands. "Look. I'm willing to let you come aboard so we can have this discussion face-to-face. I'm not willing to shut down my engines this close to Taza Four. If we drift too close, gravity is going to make this difficult for both of us. Plus, if I'm adrift without engine power, traffic control will designate me as a hazard. That comes with a bunch of paperwork I don't think you want to deal with."

"No one else is out here," Heath protested.

Hezza shrugged and tried to look innocent. "Rules are rules."

Heath pointed to someone off screen and asked. "Is she right?"

Hezza scoffed at the woman's confusion. Of *course* she was right. That was the whole reason she'd chosen this flight path.

A male voice confirmed what she already knew, and

Heath's expression turned sour. "Get yourself into a stable orbit, Captain. Then my team is coming aboard to secure you and the cargo you stole."

Hezza cocked her head to one side and tried to look puzzled instead of pissed off. "What stolen cargo?"

"The weapons," Heath hissed, her eyes suddenly filled with a vicious coldness Hezza did not like at all. "You're transporting restricted weapons that belong to the IAF."

That was *it*. "I'm doing no such thing. If by *weapons* you're referring to the two Vardarians on board the *Gambit*, they are living beings free to make their own choices. The last time I checked, the IAF didn't sanction slavery. Has that changed?"

To her credit, Heath wasn't stupid. She realized her error and backpedaled immediately.

"Of course not. But they are dangerous, and it's our stance that they need to be put into protective custody for the time being."

She was about to let loose with another volley of snark when the screen with the progress bar flashed green. A message appeared where the progress bar had been.

"Unknown device located on panel JX17-9."
Yes!

According to the scan, the tracker was on the starboard side of the ship near the midsection. Fortunately, her mates were already on the starboard side airlock. A quick tap of her fingers called up another view. This one showed Fyr'enth and Kalan in the airlock. Or it should have. Instead, all she saw was a lone figure spooling out a tether line. That would be Fyr'enth. Which meant Kalan was already on his way.

Be safe, she thought and wished she had their ability to communicate through internal channels. It was possible but only if she took the nanotech treatment. It was one more reason to add to the growing list.

Everything she'd done after her mates left the cockpit was part of the plan. Hezza was the distraction, and like every street magician or hustler she'd ever met, while she drew the mark's attention, the real work was happening somewhere else.

"Sorry for the delay, I was getting my ship repositioned so I can move it into a high orbit." What she'd actually done was ensure the starboard side of the ship remained out of the *Falcon's* line of sight while setting them up for a fast exit.

Heath's eyes narrowed even further. "Where are your Vardarian guests?" She uttered the last word with distaste.

Hezza gestured around the small cockpit. "My ship is not large. If I tried to cram my *crew* into this tiny space, I wouldn't be able to fly the ship."

"That is not an answer. If you're trying to get them off your ship..."

"To go where?" Hezza asked. "It's not like I'm going to shove them out an airlock and hope they find someone else to give them a ride."

She decided it was time to change tactics. "They're struggling to deal with everything that's happened. Your approach isn't helping the situation. Why can't you show a little empathy?"

The woman's response sent a chill down Hezza's spine. Her expression hardened, not from anger but from something worse—hatred. "I will not feel sorry for a machine. If you're not in orbit in five minutes, I will give the command to fire on you. Heath out."

The screen went blank.

"*Fraxx* you, too," Hezza muttered as she pulsed the thrusters in the general direction they were supposed to go. When it was time to get gone, she'd need every bit of acceleration she could get.

With time running out and no way to contact her mates, she was left drumming her fingers on the console as she watched Fyr'enth in the airlock. At least he was pulling the tether in, which meant Kalan was on his way back.

She was about to break radio silence and risk being overheard just to get a status update when Kalan flew through the open airlock.

Fyr'enth dropped the tether and slammed his hand down on the "seal hatch" button.

They both raised their hands and shook them at the camera so hard they looked like oversized Jeskyrans on a *ja'kreesh* bender.

She got the message. Mission accomplished.

"Ship, increase the inertial damper field in airlock one and give me full power to the standard engines with no safety checks. Once we're clear, we'll transition to hyperspace."

She'd already had the AI make the calculations on the best place to make the jump based on a specific set of criteria she'd given it. Every maneuver since then had been intended to put them on the best trajectory to reach that point in one piece. The orbital path she'd chosen put them in the *Falcon*'s line of sight, but only by a few degrees. Once she throttled up, they'd vanish behind the curve of the planet in under twenty seconds.

Heath really wasn't very good at her job. She hadn't seen what Hezza was up to, and now it was too late to stop her.

Well, it was almost too late. And that *almost* made the next twenty seconds feel like an eternity.

She considered hailing the *Falcon* to say goodbye, but rejected the idea. Taunting an enemy with more guns than you was never a good idea.

Instead, she throttled up the engines and flew like her life depended on it... because it did.

CHAPTER 19

Even with the inertial dampeners on, Kalan found himself staggering as he fought to keep his balance when the *Gambit* accelerated.

He tried to spread his wings, but they were clamped to his back by the EVA suit he wore.

He'd almost forgotten about that while he was moving along the hull of the ship. Being out in the void, with nothing but blackness in every direction, was almost like flying.

Once the ship's acceleration smoothed out, he unlatched his helmet and removed it. Zero-G was fun, but having his head crammed inside a helmet with a limited field of vision and stale-tasting air hadn't been enjoyable.

"What was it like?" Fyr'enth asked once he had his own helmet off.

"The sims were mostly accurate. The views are better, though. Open sky in all directions instead of one. It was more disorienting than I had expected. It felt like I was falling much of the time, and I couldn't use my wings."

"I felt the same thing every time I looked out the hatch. We'll have to find out what adaptations the Vardarians use for their suits. No doubt we'll learn more than we want once we reach Haven."

They'd talked via their internal link the whole time Kalan was outside the ship and had agreed that the colony was the obvious choice. That made things problematic too. Even if the plan worked and they could stop the tracker from sending a signal, the ones chasing them would have to come to the same conclusion. If they left messages before leaving this system, it was possible, even likely, that the IAF would beat them to the colony. In fact, they probably had ships on their way there already.

It meant they'd be flying into a dangerous situation.

He grinned as he began freeing himself from the EVA suit. Danger had been their constant companion since they'd met their *mahaya*. He wasn't worried about himself or his brother. And if he won the argument he knew was coming, he would be less concerned about Hezza, too.

By the time they'd stowed their gear, Hezza had announced they'd made the transition to hyperspace. "We're clear for now, but there's not a snowball's chance in a supernova that they're not following us."

"Did they fire on us?" Fyr'enth asked.

If they had, Kalan hadn't detected any indication the shots had actually hit the ship.

"They did, but I've been dodging weapons fire longer

than that crew has been alive. Their gunner used the same standard firing patterns every gunner learns during their first year of training." She sounded pleased and relieved, but he didn't miss the note of strain still in her voice. Their escape hadn't been as easy as she claimed.

"When you're ready, meet me in the galley. We've got cinnamon bites to eat and plans to discuss."

"We'll be there shortly," Kalan said. Then he turned to his brother and spoke via their internal comms. *"We're still in agreement about our zana?"*

"We are."

"Then I'll grab what we need on the way to the galley."

"See you there."

He walked into the galley with a small bag slung over his shoulder. Inside were the items they needed, though there was still some question of whether Hezza would be agreeable.

If she argued, they had a plan for how to convince her to change her mind. It involved sweet talk and orgasms.

"Are you contributing to the stack of snacks?" Hezza asked. A bowl full of the sugar-dusted morsels they'd brought back to the ship sat in front of her along with three mugs of his new favorite beverage—hot cocoa topped with marshmallows.

"This?" He patted the bag before setting it down on the floor near his stool and taking a seat. "Contains a gift for you, but I am afraid it's not food."

"Then I'll have to have another one of these." Hezza picked up one of the cinnamon bites. "Grab one before they're gone."

Fyr'enth offered him the bowl. "Take two. They're delicious. Hezza told me that the version our food dispenser makes is not half as good."

"We need to get a better model. One that can make pizza, too," Kalan said before popping one into his mouth.

"It's not the model that's the problem. It's the ingredients. I don't know how he does it, but Flek always sources the best of everything for his food, and it's fresh. That's not easy to do on a ship."

"Then why don't we get our supplies from Flek?" Fyr'enth asked.

Kalan wanted to know the answer, too, but he was too busy enjoying this new taste experience to ask.

Hezza opened her mouth, but for several seconds she didn't say anything.

"Huh. That is a damn good question. And it gives me an idea about how I can pay him back for the favors I currently owe him."

"What favors?" Kalan asked.

"While you two were getting the tracker off the hull of my ship, I sent him another message. I've got no doubt he'll come through for us, but it won't be easy."

"What did you ask him to do?" Fyr'enth asked. This wasn't something they'd had time to discuss before they had to enact their part of the plan.

"I asked him to add more messages." Her expression turned serious. "We can't fend these assholes off forever.

If we have to face them, I want to stack the odds in our favor as much as I can."

"Makes sense," Kalan agreed.

Fyr'enth placed the tracker on the table between them. "Before we talk about the future, we need to deal with this."

Hezza nodded and then spoke in the tone she used when addressing the AI. "Hey, ship. Is the item I asked you to fabricate ready yet?"

"It is."

"Good. Have a bot bring it to the galley."

"Request confirmed. It will arrive in thirty-seven seconds."

"Is this the shielded container you mentioned earlier?" Kalan asked around another mouthful of sugary bliss.

"Yeah. Now that the AI has had a chance to scan it, it can detect the signal. I'm not an expert on this kind of thing, but from what I understand, the signal it gave off blended with the ambient noise generated by the ship. Very sneaky." She tapped the tracker with a finger. "Now we know about it, I think we should keep it muted until we can use it to our advantage."

Kalan immediately saw her intent. "You want to reactive it once we're on our way to the colony on Liberty. We can turn their own trap against them."

"If everyone gets my message and follows through? Then, yeah, that's the plan. Do either of you have any objections?"

"None," Kalan said.

"Me either," Fyr'enth said.

"Then that's the plan. When we get to Haven, we'll find out if anyone accepted my invitation." She smiled at them. "That's what I asked Flek to do. I sent an open invitation to every being I consider a friend. We're going to Liberty, and if we're lucky, we'll have allies waiting when we get there."

"How long will they need to get there?"

"Some of them could be there in a few days. Others will need two weeks. Until then, we're going to have to keep moving. Without the tracker, the *Falcon* might give up the chase, but we can't know for certain without letting them catch up. I don't want to do that."

"Neither do we," Kalan agreed. Today they'd been lucky. If they were caught a second time? No, it was best they didn't take that risk.

Fyr'enth stood. "It's a good plan. But there's something we can do to make it better."

Kalan got to his feet, too. "Come with us, Alyssa."

"But we still have cinnamon bites," she complained.

Kalan scooped the bag off the floor. "They can wait a little while. Or don't you want to know what's in here?"

"I think I'm getting hustled."

"We learned from the best," Kalan said without bothering to hide his smug grin.

They led her to her cabin, though it was really *their* cabin now. They'd only spent one long, lonely night sleeping in their own quarters.

Once inside, Kalan pulled out the three items contained in the bag, though he held them in one hand and hid it behind his back.

"What have you got there?" Hezza tried to lean to one side to get a glimpse of what he held.

There wasn't much room in the cabin, but they managed to find the space to stand in front of her.

"We have something for you, Alyssa," Kalan said. "If we were truly Vardarian, this would be a *harani*." He named the traditional armband mated triads wore to display their status. "But since we're not, we've created a new tradition."

With that, he held out the smallest of the three wrist cuffs they had made.

Hezza exhaled sharply, her eyes locked on the piece of hammered metal he held out to her.

"Is that..." She leaned down to look closer. "You made this out of a part of a hull patch kit?"

Before he could answer, she took it out of his hand with a soft sound of unmistakable delight. "You did!" She examined it carefully, her eyes bright and her smile wider than he'd ever seen it.

She liked it. That was good. But would she put it on?

"There's an inscription," Fyr'enth said. "On the inside."

She turned it so that the light shone at the right angle. "For our *zana*. Our lives began the day we met you."

She blinked rapidly, and her voice cracked with emotion as she turned toward them. "This is perfect. Thank you."

Then she slipped it onto her wrist. "I accept your gift and everything it represents."

"You are our *mahaya*. Now everyone will know it," Kalan said.

She laughed. "Oh yes, they will. And if they don't see this, I'll tell them myself. I'm spoken for."

She held out her hand. "Please tell me you made some for yourselves, too."

Pleased to the point of bursting, he handed her the two larger cuffs. They were identical to hers, except for the size. All three were cut from the same piece of metal, and then hammered into the proper shape. They'd done more hammering to add a decorative design to the outside, and then polished them to a brilliant shine.

"What do yours say?" she asked.

"That is for you to decide," Fyr'enth said.

"I supposed just putting the word *mine*, in big letters would be too much?"

"Probably." Kalan bared his teeth. "Or you could just growl at them the way you did at Sajita. That seemed to work well."

"It did. Didn't it? Then I'll think of something meaningful to engrave instead." She placed a cuff on his wrist and then Fyr'enth's. Once fitted, they covered the bar codes tattooed on their flesh.

That felt right.

"You are my *mahoyen*," she declared when it was done. "Always."

"Always. Do you mean that, Alyssa?" he asked softly.

"I do. I once asked you to give me more time before we talked about the nanotech again. You gave me that time, and I want to give you my answer now."

He held his breath. Maybe they wouldn't need to ply her with pleasure after all. They'd still do that, of course, but for different reasons.

"What is your answer?" Fyr'enth asked impatiently.

The corners of her mouth lifted in amusement. "Impatient, are we? Very well. During the time you were both in the void and I was safe inside... Well, relatively safe... I realized I'd do anything to keep us together. Even die. That made my choice easy. My answer is yes."

"Finally." Kalan took her hand and dusted several light kisses to her fingers.

"It wasn't that long!" she protested with a laugh that made his heart fill with emotions he was finally ready to name.

"I love you, Alyssa Bratt. My *mahaya*."

"Our beautiful *zana*, the mate we were always destined to find." Fyr'enth moved in and took her in his arms for a long, heated kiss.

Kalan watched them, expecting to feel the teeth of jealousy take hold, but it never happened. His heart and soul filled with a soft, warm light. It was more than love. More than happiness. It was a feeling only one being in the universe could provide—their *mahaya*.

He stripped off his clothes and let them fall to the floor in a pile. He'd tidy up later. Right now, he had more important things to do.

"My turn," he said when his brother finally raised his head to breathe.

"This is why I need your nanotech. How else am I going to keep up with the two of you?" Hezza laughed as she spoke, her skin flushed and eyes bright with desire.

"That was the third argument on my list." Fyr'enth released their mate and stepped back to take off his own clothes.

"You had a list?" Hezza asked, her expression somewhere between bemused and surprised.

He folded her into his arms and grinned down at her. "We did. We were prepared for you to be stubborn."

"I resemble that remark," she admitted and rose on her toes to kiss him. He bowed his head to meet her halfway and groaned when her lips met his.

It was like this every time. Even now, days after the *sharhal* had first taken hold. Reading about the mating fever and its lasting effects was one thing, but experiencing it was something else again. The spark between them would never go out.

She surprised him by reaching down to stroke his hard, aching cock. He groaned into her mouth, rocking his hips against the soft touch of her hand.

"I want you," he murmured several dizzying kisses later.

"We want you," Fyr'enth said. He stood to one side, his hand on their mate's hip.

"Then we should do something about that." She tipped her head to one side, baring her throat. "Because I believe I was promised mating marks."

The sight made his cock throb. *Yes.* His fangs lengthened just thinking about it.

"Clothes off. Now." He spoke without thinking.

She simply laughed and began to unfasten the clasps on her jumpsuit.

"I hate these things," he muttered as he reached up to help.

"They don't come off easily," Fyr'enth agreed.

"But they do protect me from dirt, burns, and chemical spills," she pointed out.

"Once you have our nanotech, you won't need to worry about the last two," Kalan reminded her.

"And if you get dirty, your *mahoyen* will be happy to help you get clean," Fyr'enth added.

"If that's the case, we're going to need a bigger shower." Hezza raised her arms to allow Kalan to pull her T-shirt over her head.

"Hells, we're going to need to reconfigure the cabin space and the cockpit. I love you both, but you're too *fraxxing* big for my ship."

"A bigger bed would be nice," Kalan agreed. Then he lifted her off the deck, holding her suspended while Fyr'enth tugged off the last of her clothes.

Without a word of warning, he took two steps straight back and then let himself fall onto the bed that filled one end of the cabin.

Hezza squeaked in surprise but didn't tense or brace herself for impact. She trusted him to protect her. As she should.

She was their treasure. Their *mahaya*. Their *everything*.

CHAPTER 20

T\ʟ\ʟ\Tᴜᴍʙʟɪɴɢ onto the bed might have been uncomfortable, but among the many adjustments they'd made to what had once been her private cabin was an area of lowered gravity around their bed.

With less force drawing them onto the mattress, her mates found it easier to sleep comfortably. Their wings were a feat of bioengineering, but they differed from the original design and couldn't be folded against their bodies the same way.

Not that their creators cared if they were comfortable. All they'd been concerned with was their viability as weapons. They were so much more than that, and she would keep finding ways to make this cold, uncaring universe more welcoming for them.

That was the last clear thought she had. Once they landed, she found herself sprawled on top of a very naked, very aroused male who had no interest in letting her go.

"*Mahaya*," he said the word like it was a prayer and a

compliment rolled into one. His hand cupped the back of her head, pulling her down for a slow, sizzling kiss that made her toes curl and her blood boil. His mouth ravaged hers, the tips of his fangs grazing her lips. Those teeth were sharp enough to draw blood, and soon, they'd do just that. At first, the idea alarmed her. Now? Now she couldn't wait for it to happen.

Hezza deliberately rubbed her pussy over Kalan's hard shaft, capturing his next groan against her lips. His kisses grew harder, his tongue plunging into her mouth.

She felt the mattress dip as Fyr'enth joined them. When his hands stroked her back, they were already slick with *uli* oil. As he traced patterns across her skin, he left tingling trails in his wake. As he moved his hands lower, she moaned, anticipating what would happen soon.

An oil-slick hand slipped between her body and Kalan's, seeking out her nipples one at a time. Every tweak and touch added to her arousal. In a matter of seconds, she was writhing between them as they caressed her with hard, urgent hands.

Fyr'enth guided her onto her hands and knees so that Kalan was between her thighs. It also meant there was a gap between her pussy and Kalan's cock. Enough space for Fyr'enth to use his fingers to coat her pussy with the oil, making several tight circles around her clit.

Kalan uttered a groan as some of the oil dripped off Fyr'enth's hand and onto his cock.

"Oops." Fyr'enth didn't sound the slightest bit sorry.

"You'll pay for that," Kalan grumbled.

Hezza kissed Kalan to distract him and then turned

to look over her shoulder at Fyr'enth as he kneeled behind her, still strumming her clit with his fingers.

She shivered and bucked against his touch. She ached with need, not for one cock but for two. She wanted them both inside her, and she needed it soon.

Fyr'enth worked her clit hard for several strokes, bringing her to the brink of orgasm before pulling his hand away.

She lowered herself onto Kalan's cock a second later, earning herself a grin from the male lying beneath her.

"I think our *zana* is ready." Kalan arched himself beneath her to let his cock slide between her folds, the oil making everything more intense.

"Do you want my cock?" he asked in a voice gone rough with need.

"You know the answer to that will always be yes."

"I do. But I like hearing you say it." He released her breast and reached between them, seating the thick head of his cock at her opening.

She didn't wait for him to move his hand but drove herself down on his cock, taking him balls deep inside her.

"Qarf!" Kalan's hips snapped up, lifting her off the mattress.

Hezza's mind and body were bombarded with sensations so intense they threatened to overwhelm her. Her skin burned as her pussy throbbed and pulsed around Kalan's cock.

Behind her, Fyr'enth worked his fingers into the cleft of her ass, more oil coating his fingers as he slowly worked his way deeper.

When he penetrated her from behind, she stiffened, not with pain but a new, darker kind of pleasure. He worked her slowly open, each press of his fingers driving her down onto Kalan's cock.

The tempo slowed as the intensity increased, riding wave after wave of pleasure.

When Fyr'enth pulled his hand away this time, she knew what would happen next. Despite herself, she tensed and uttered a low, needy moan.

Kalan touched her cheek, drawing her attention back to him. "I love you, Alyssa," he whispered.

"And I love you, Kalan. And you, Fyr'enth. Everything I am, everything I have, belongs to you both."

Fyr'enth pressed himself against her back opening, easing himself slowly into the tight ring of her ass. After a bite of pain that faded into pleasure, she was truly caught between them.

Hezza could do nothing but let them love her, each of them moving in turn and taking her to the peaks of ecstasy. One would enter as the other retreated.

"Our *zana* is so beautiful," Fyr'enth murmured, his hands on her hips as he fucked her.

"Yes, she is," Kalan agreed.

On the last word, he raised his head to kiss the side of her throat. Only it was more than a kiss. As his fangs broke the skin, Fyr'enth leaned over her, claiming the other side of her neck.

Hezza's world exploded into crystalline bliss. Her senses shattered as an orgasm stronger than she'd ever experienced tore through her. She lost herself in a sea of pleasure, her body clamping down on both males as they came along with her.

She collapsed onto Kalan with a deep, contented sigh, her body still rocked by aftershocks and her heart overflowing with love.

"Mine," she murmured dazedly, barely aware of the word coming out of her mouth.

"Ours," Fyr'enth agreed, his breath tickling the back of her neck.

"Always," Kalan said as he stroked her cheek with his fingertips.

She let herself linger in post-coital bliss as long as she could. The galaxy was still full of dangers, but for this one, brief moment, her life was closer to perfect than she'd ever imagined it could be.

It was more than she deserved, but that didn't matter anymore. Her lovers had made their choice, and she'd made hers.

CHAPTER 21

Tʜᴇʏ ᴡᴇʀᴇ all in the cockpit when the time came to transit back to normal space. Hezza was beside him with Kalan seated at the weapons station, his hands on the controls. If they were met by hostiles, they'd be ready.

Fyr'enth hoped that wouldn't be the case. He wanted his first view of Liberty and its colony to happen without being tainted by violence.

"Do you think anyone came?" Hezza sounded worried, and her fingers were drumming a staccato beat on the edge of the console.

He placed his hand over hers and squeezed it lightly. "I think your friends are waiting for you. Whoever shows up, it will be enough."

At the very least, he expected Phylomenia and her males to be in the system. Would anyone else be there? That depended on how long it took her messages to reach them and how far they'd had to travel. They'd taken the *Gambit* on a tour of the most isolated places she could think of. Sometimes, they'd take the tracker out and let it drop its breadcrumbs into the void. Other times, they'd kept it locked away. No one had caught up with them, so their tactics had worked well enough.

They'd traveled for the better part of three weeks, avoiding all but the most remote outposts. The few times they'd stopped to restock supplies, they'd gone to automated way stations where the odds of crossing paths with another ship were slim.

"I hope you're right." Hezza tapped the screen, and a countdown timer appeared. In five seconds, they'd drop to normal space and find out who was waiting for them.

Three. Two. One.

"Holy *fraxx*," Hezza stared at the viewscreen in shock.

Green lights lit up the display, each one indicating a friendly vessel.

There were a handful of red lights, too, but they were almost lost in the sea of emerald.

"I have four—no, five IAF ships on visual. Four are in orbit around the third planet in the system. One appears to be patrolling the outer areas."

"We are being hailed," the ship's AI announced.

"By whom?" Hezza asked.

Instead of answering verbally, a list of names appeared on a smaller monitor. It took him a split second to realize each entry was a ship name and the name of the being making the call.

The Bat Out of Hell 2—Phylomenia Harrington
The Sun Sprite—Zura Watson

The Alacrity V—Tianna Astor
The Santar—Prince Tyran of Haven Colony

"Are you *qarfing* kidding me? How am I supposed to pick who to talk to first?"

"Talk to Phylomenia. We know her," Kalan suggested.

Fyr'enth recognized all the names but only because he'd read as much as he could find about the cyborg rebellion and what came afterward. He knew about the Gray Men and their evolution into a new threat now called the Shadows. Zura Watson and Tianna were mentioned in those files, but he wasn't sure why they were here, so he discounted them as options.

Given the choice between Phylomenia and the unknown Vardarian prince, he agreed with Kalan. The human was the better bet.

Hezza opened a channel. "Hey, Phyl. It's good to see you. I wasn't expecting things to be so, uh, crowded around here."

Phylomenia's face appeared a second later. She looked the same as the last time Fyr'enth had seen her, only her smile seemed brighter this time.

"You made it! We were worried some asshat IAF officer had done something stupid," she said in her gentle drawl.

"You're just saying that to rile up your husbands. And, no, we didn't see anyone on our little tour, IAF or otherwise. Not until we arrived here, anyway. Is that Barrios's task force I see in orbit?"

"It is." Phylomenia smirked. "He's been trying to give orders to everyone, even the prince. To say it hasn't gone well for him is putting it mildly. Scott's sent so many letters of complaint I'm amazed no one's been sent to replace him yet."

"Any sign of the *Falcon?*" Fyr'enth asked.

"*Fraxx*, you two cleaned up nicely. Apologies for the question, but are you Fyr'enth or Kalan? And to answer your question, the *Falcon* is in the system, but Barrios is being cagey about its whereabouts."

"I'm Fyr'enth," he said. It felt good to have another being use his chosen name.

"Nice to see you again. Both of you." She gave Hezza a long, intense look. "So? Are they your mates or not?"

Hezza laughed. Then she turned her head from side to side to show off the marks on either side of her neck.

"Yes! Congratulations to all three of you. Anya sends her love, by the way. She's waiting for you to contact her, but she figured you'd be swamped with messages when you first arrived."

"She's the next one I'm contacting after this," Hezza said.

"Maybe make that the second one you call. Prince Tyran needs to speak to you. It's important, Hez. You wouldn't believe how intense things have been lately. Haven is on high alert, and a lot of the ships you're seeing are Vardarian cruisers. The news about the new cyborgs hit them hard, and they're ready to start a war if anyone does something foolish. Now that you and your mates are here, we've got a chance to get things hammered out."

"I can do that. But there's not much more we can tell them that wasn't on the files I sent."

"They need to talk to Kalan and Fyr'enth. All the other cyborgs are still in cryo-pods."

"Why haven't they been woken up yet?" Fyr'enth asked. As far as he was concerned, cryo was just another kind of prison.

"Getting Barrios to release them took longer than it should have. I don't understand why, but he finally agreed to the transfer two days ago. They're down on the surface now, well-protected and being examined by our medical staff and healers. They'll be awake soon, but there were some concerns that the pods might be trapped in some way."

"That's possible?" Kalan asked.

Phylomenia looked grim. "It is."

Hezza nodded. "They did it before. At the end of the cyborg rebellion. When they knew it was over and the cyborgs would be freed, some of the corporations sabotaged the cryo-pods so that if the proper codes weren't used during deactivation, the cyborg inside died."

"What about the staff who fled the research station and were captured? Have they told you anything?"

"It's been frustrating. The only ones who want to talk don't know much. They've given us the names of their superiors, but we don't have many of them in custody, and they aren't cooperating."

Phylomenia made a soft sound at the back of her throat. "I do have some news for you. The Pheran female who gave you the data stick was last seen boarding one of the ships that was shot down while trying to leave. I'm sorry. She wasn't one of the survivors."

A pang of sorrow hit Fyr'enth harder than he expected. He'd barely known the female, but in a place full of cruelty, she'd been one of a handful to never do him or Kalan harm.

"Thank you for telling us," he said.

"Did you find out anything about Detta Ani? The Vardarian in charge of the research station?" Kalan asked.

"No news there, either. The Vardarians are still looking, but so far they can't find any information with that name or likeness." Phylomenia sighed. "I wish I had something positive to tell you. There's so much we don't know right now, and it worries me." Phylomenia tugged at her hair absently and then sighed.

"This feels too much like what happened on Astek Station. All the models predict that the Shadows are too fractured to do any real damage, but this..." She shrugged. "This feels like their handiwork. When we are done here, we're escorting Tianna and Zura's ships back to Defiance Station. I don't want anyone I care about flying around alone out there right now." Phylomenia smiled and added, "Consider that an invitation to make the trip with us. I don't know what your plans are, but you know you can always find work in The Drift."

"I can't say yes right now, but I do appreciate the invitation." Hezza raised a hand in a gesture of goodbye. "Talk to you soon."

The call ended, leaving the cockpit in silence.

• • •

"I'm sorry about the Pheran female. I know she wasn't really a friend, but still, she deserved better," Hezza said.

"She did," Fyr'enth agreed.

"Maybe she's at peace now. I don't think she had much of that on the station," Kalan said.

"I hope so." Hezza sat up straighter and drew in a long breath. "Are you two ready to meet the prince? He should be our next call."

"No," Fyr'enth said.

"Not even a little. But it has to be done," Kalan agreed.

"Yeah, it does. But before we do that, I want you to know something."

She pivoted her chair around to face them both, her knees crammed against his thigh. "I love you, and no matter what happens next, we'll get through it. Together."

She held out her hands to them, and Fyr'enth took one as his brother took the other.

"Together," they said at the same time.

"Okay then. Let's talk to the prince and see what he has to say."

"And if we don't like what we hear?" Fyr'enth asked the question weighing heavily on his mind.

"Then we fight until we get the answers we want," Kalan said, his voice dangerously calm.

"Agreed," Hezza said and squeezed their hands.

Fyr'enth looked at this beautiful, brave, enthralling female and knew in his heart that things would go their way. How could they not when they had their *mahaya* standing with them?

CHAPTER 22

THE DOCKING CLAMPS hadn't even finished attaching when the alert sounded. "Another vessel has entered the system. Identity confirmed as the *Falcon*."

Kalan cursed. "Should I target lock them? Or do you think that will annoy everyone?"

"It will definitely piss off a few people, but I'm tempted to say yes anyway," Hezza said and tapped a finger to her chin. It would be *so* satisfying, but it wasn't worth the problems that would result.

"But we don't need to make things more difficult. Let the prince and the leadership council handle this. It's their system."

To her amusement, Kalan actually pouted for a second. "If you say so."

They stayed in their seats to watch as two with transponder codes that marked them as part of Liberty's defense force broke orbit and flew on an intercept course, straight for the new arrival.

"She's not going to be happy about that," Fyr'enth said.

"Good," Kalan muttered.

"As much as I'd love to stay and watch, we need to get going," she reminded them. "The prince was clear he wants us to attend this meeting."

"Do you think this empress will be there?" Fyr'enth asked.

"I expect so." It had been a surprise to them all to learn that the empress had taken Hezza's invitation seriously and come in person. Her flagship was docked at the orbital platform, looking as sleek and dangerous as any ship she'd ever seen. Barrios must have lost his mind when the Vardarian battle cruiser had arrived and messed up his attempts to dictate terms to Tyran and the leadership council.

Their conversation with the prince had been brief but friendly. He'd seemed delighted to speak to Kalan and Fyr'enth, and he treated them with honesty and respect.

They hadn't said much beforehand, but she sensed they'd been concerned that Tyran would treat them as curiosities or some kind of threat. Now she felt like they were prepared to trust him, and that was all she could ask for.

Once they'd learned about the meeting, they'd spent what little time they had during the transit to the orbital platform to shower and change. For this event, they'd need to look their best.

She wore the most formal attire she owned—a pair of

black pants with a flowing, forest green top made of *keski* silk. It was sleeveless with a crossover neckline that flattered her shape and put her new wrist cuff on full display.

Her mates had rejected her suggestion that they wear a Vardarian-style top. Instead, they both wore black pants, their usual boots, and a simple black sash that went over one shoulder, across their chest, and ended at the hip. Their only embellishment was the wrist cuff they each wore.

"You look good. I mean, really good. Maybe I should enroll you both in acting classes and try to get you contracts as holo-vid performers. We could live a life of luxury," she joked as they made their way to the hatch.

"And give up the *Gambit?* Never," Fyr'enth said.

"The only eyes I want watching me are yours, *zana*," Kalan said.

"Very smooth, Kal. Ten out of ten for content and delivery. Just please don't try to charm the empress. I don't want her thinking she can take you away from me."

"She can't," they both stated at the same time.

Stars above and below, she loved them.

The prince waited near the hatchway. With him were his *anrik*, Braxon, and their human *mahaya*, Phaedra. For once, the cyber-jockey turned princess looked entirely serious. Even her fuchsia-colored hair was tied back in an elaborate braid.

"Thank you for meeting us. We could have found our way there on our own." Hezza bowed her head to acknowledge the prince and his consorts.

"And miss the opportunity to meet your mates before everyone else? Not a chance." Phaedra beamed at Kalan and Fyr'enth. "Hi. I'm Phaedra. This is Braxon, and you've spoken to Tyr already. This meeting will probably have too many speeches and not enough snacks, but don't worry too much. Whatever happens, we've got your back."

Kalan blinked down at her in surprise. Hezza didn't blame him. Phaedra was a breath of fresh air in any situation, but her open demeanor and total lack of formality took some getting used to.

"Hello." Kalan looked over at Hezza. "You didn't tell us about her hair."

"No, I didn't. It's part of the Phaedra experience." She grinned as Phaedra laughed.

"I like that! The Phaedra experience. I'm going to steal that if you don't mind."

"Of course."

After that, things were easier. They chatted about inconsequential matters as they walked through the station. The prince had mentioned his intention to take them on a bit of a tour. Not so much to show the station to her mates but to let the colonists see the new arrivals.

Fyr'enth and Kalan didn't enjoy all the attention, but she understood the prince's reasons. The colonists were curious, and it was better for them to see for themselves instead of gossip and conjecture filling in the gaps.

Everywhere they went, beings stopped and stared at Kalan and Fyr'enth. Some waved to Phaedra or bowed to the prince, but most of them couldn't take their eyes off the new arrivals.

"It's your wings," Phaedra said. "They're beautiful but very different from what everyone is used to seeing."

"They'll get used to it," Braxon said and then frowned slightly. "Apologies. They'll get used to it if you decide to stay on Haven."

"You are welcome to stay," Tyran said. "You could make a home here, but in your case, I imagine you already have another offer." The prince smiled at Hezza. "With your *mahaya*."

Kalan turned to look at Hezza and mouthed a single word. "Smooth."

She had to fake a cough to hide her laughter.

Over time, the males began to talk among themselves. That gave Hezza an opportunity to talk to Phaedra alone. She fell back a meter or so, not enough to be obvious, and lowered her voice while keeping the tone conversational.

"How bad is this going to be?" she asked.

"Tyran wants to tie the Barrios idiot up in his own red tape and kick him out an airlock, and he's normally the diplomatic one. The colonel keeps trying to pull rank and make demands as if this was a human colony or somewhere under corporate control."

"How's the empress taking it?"

"About as well as you'd think. Neha is proud, stubborn, and can be a bit of a bitch, but that might be my bias talking. Our first meeting was not a good one, and I am known for holding a grudge. I think her biggest problem is that she's spent most of her life surrounded by sycophants and courtiers currying favor. Tyran likes to say that she rules by committee, and I have to agree with him. The thing is, the committee she relies on for advice is full of assholes."

"How is she dealing with the news that her own citizens have been cloned and experimented on?" Hezza needed to know what they were walking into, and so far, it wasn't sounding good.

"She's livid. So is Tyran. At first, we all assumed the DNA came from Haven, but we've done biopsies on the cyborgs in cryo, and none of them are a match to the beings here."

"That means the donors are citizens of the empire?"

Phaedra nodded. "Most likely. Yes. And some of them are shedding their scales about it. It's pretty easy to tell who is sympathetic to the Liq'za when they keep going on about the risk of tainting the *genetic perfection* of the Vardarian race. For some of these beings, it is more upsetting to think that the old bloodlines might have been mixed with inferior families than the idea of someone being cloned and enslaved."

Now came the dangerous question. "Is the empress one of those beings?"

To her relief, Phaedra shook her head. "I don't think so. But she's adopted some of the terms. Tyran is beside himself about it. They've never seen eye-to-eye on everything, but this is new. Their mother used to run interference, but she didn't accompany Neha this time. I get the feeling some of her companions convinced her she needed to do this on her own. Which of course, really meant they could influence her without her mother being around to stop it."

"What is she going to do with the cyborgs? The new ones?"

Phaedra flashed a tight smile. "I wish I knew. The one thing I am certain about is that she has no intention of letting the IAF or any corporation have them."

"That's a good start."

"It's something," Phaedra agreed. "One more thing before we get inside. Neha wasn't ready to take the throne when their father died. She thought she had more time. Decades more. She wanted Tyran to stay and help her lead their people. He refused because he knew she needed to stand on her own or she'd never let him leave."

Hezza nodded. "I've heard the stories. I know she wasn't thrilled about his relationship with Braxon or that his mate is human."

"Neha isn't a terrible being, but she's struggling to find her way right now, and that's causing problems. She adores her niece, though, and she's warming up to me, so there is hope. She's been fed a lot of poison. I'm just not sure how we help her see that."

Hezza had several suggestions, but they ran out of time before she could voice them, which was probably for the best. A pointy-toed boot planted in the imperial derriere was not exactly a diplomatic solution.

Two Vardarian guards in body armor emblazoned with a crest she didn't recognize bowed to the prince and then stepped aside, letting them pass through a pair of double doors and into a medium-sized meeting room.

It was a relatively mundane space with a simple blue patterned carpet, white walls, and the high ceilings typical of Vardarian architecture. Several long tables had been set up in a line across the far end of the room, and a number of beings were already seated.

She recognized Denz, Raze, and all the other members of Haven's leadership council. Seated at the far end was Barrios and a small group of IAF officers, all in dress uniform. Seated beside the colonel was an unexpected surprise. Lieutenant Commander Heath.

"What's *she* doing here?" Hezza hissed at Phaedra.

Tyran, whose hearing was almost as good as a cyborg, heard her question and quickly realized who Hezza meant.

He scowled, flared his wings slightly, and gestured toward the group of IAF members. "Why is Lieutenant Commander Heath here? She's already threatened my guests once already."

Barrios stiffened. "She is my second in command. Any interaction she had with that woman and those mach..." He cut himself off and started again. "Prince Tyran. You said I could choose who could accompany me to this meeting. Once I learned she was in the system, I asked her to join me as soon as possible."

Hezza had never been in the presence of someone who actually had an aura of power about them. Tyran did. All eyes were on him as he considered the colonel's answer. She could feel the disapproval radiating from in waves as he stared for several long seconds at the colonel and his party.

"I will hold you accountable for her behavior, and when this meeting is over, I expect her to depart immediately and return to your ship."

"I...yes. Of course. She'll leave when I do." Barrios sat back in his chair, almost vibrating with unspoken outrage.

With that dealt with, Hezza checked out the rest of the guests. In the center of the table was a female Vardarian who had to be Empress Neha. She had silver scales and gemstones woven into her long, dark hair.

"Sister," Tyran spoke in a loud, polished tone as he approached the table. "I have brought Captain Bratt and the two cyborg prisoners she freed to meet with you."

There were audible gasps and murmurs from the Vardarians seated on either side of the empress. Hezza assumed these were her advisors.

Even without augmented hearing, she caught the word *abomination* muttered several times.

Kalan and Fyr'enth had moved to flank her as they entered, and now they spread their wings protectively, forming a shield across all their backs.

Neha ignored the outburst and rose to her feet. Her smile was as perfect as the rest of her, but it also seemed genuine, if a little uncertain.

Phaedra was right. This empress lacked confidence. Never a good thing in a leader.

"You are welcome," Neha said. "I am Neha, your empress."

Both of her escorts came to a halt. "I am Kalan. This is Fyr'enth. We appreciate your welcome, but we want to make something clear. We are not your subjects."

This time, the masks slipped, and several of the courtiers shot her *mahoyen* ugly, hate-filled looks.

"What?" Neha stammered but then composed herself. "Explain yourselves."

As much as it pained her, Hezza stayed quiet. This was something that her mates had to do themselves. If she spoke for them, she'd rob them of their chance to speak their truth and set the terms for everything that came after.

Fyr'enth spoke next. "Our genetics may be Vardarian, but we are not from your empire. We were not raised there, and we have no understanding of your culture or values. We are cyborgs, and we claim that as our lineage. While some of us may wish to become your subjects in the future, my brother and I do not."

"This is unexpected." Neha's eyes were narrowed and her lips were pressed thin, but she seemed more confused than anything else.

Barrios spoke next. "You heard them. They denied that they were Vardarian. Therefore, they cannot claim the empire's protection. That means my claim for custody should be acknowledged."

"No," Kalan and Fyr'enth spoke together.

Hezza couldn't tell if they were addressing the empress, the colonel, or both at once.

A female Hezza had never seen before stood up from the table. She'd been seated by the leadership council, but she wasn't one of the members. She was tall for a human, but then Hezza caught the glint of something metal beneath the fall of her chestnut hair. Was she a cyborg?

"I think you all need to hear what I've got to say. First, I should introduce myself. My name is Chance, and I'm a cyborg with a specific skill set. Unlike my brethren,

I wasn't made to fight wars." She smiled sadly. "I was made to predict who would win them."

Chance. Hezza knew the name and the story of the cyborg it belonged to. She'd left Haven early, fleeing back to a space station where her agoraphobia wouldn't be triggered every time she stepped outside her door. Chance had found her way to The Drift and Astek Station, where she'd joined with other members of the cyborg resistance.

"I know who you are." Barrios sneered. "And what you are. Why are you here?"

"I was invited." She indicated the group from Haven. "They know me and my abilities. They asked me to come here and help them with this situation. I can do calculations that no one else can, and I've finished my analysis." She looked at Hezza, and her smile widened. "I really think you should listen to what I have to say."

"Speak," Neha said. Then she looked chagrined. "Sorry, brother. I forgot my place. This is your domain, not mine."

Tyran waved her apology off. "I'd like to hear what Chance has to say, too."

"As you all know, DNA samples were taken from the Vardarian cyborgs still in cryo-pods. Upon their arrival, Kalan and Fyr'enth were also asked to provide samples. I have the results, and they match my predictions. All the cyborgs recovered from Orio Station carry DNA from multiple Vardarian sources. However, one of them is relevant to the several parties present today. Every cyborg removed from the station carries genetic material from the Varosa family line. Tyran and Neha, I would like to introduce you to the newest members of your family."

Family? Hezza had expected things to get complicated over the course of this meeting, but she'd never imagined *this*.

"We have family?" Fyr'enth's question was more whisper than sound.

Around them, questions were shouted, and several Vardarians protested in obvious outrage.

It was hard to hear through the chaos, but she heard words like *travesty*, *abomination*, and others just as vile.

Finally, Tyran had had enough. "This is a family matter!" His voice boomed like thunder. "Everyone else leave!"

He quickly turned to Chance and added, "Thank you, Chance. We'll talk soon."

"Of course." The cyborg moved away, shadowed by a blond, dangerous-looking human male.

"I'm not leaving until I get some answers!" Barrios's voice had risen to something uncomfortably close to a toddler's wail when they didn't get the cookie they wanted.

He'd left the table with the rest of his group but had stopped not far from where Hezza and her group stood. Most of his officers continued toward the door, but not the lieutenant commander. She stood by Barrios, whispering to him with one hand on his arm.

Interesting. There was something between the first officer and her commander that should not exist between two beings in their positions.

"Do you see what I see?" Phaedra asked.

"I do. That might explain why the first officer of the *Bright Arrow* was able to commandeer someone else's ship to come after us."

The room emptied relatively quickly. Even the other Vardarians grudgingly departed, herded out a side door by more of the empress's guards.

"Colonel Barrios, I asked you to leave." Tyran glowered at the smaller male.

"I have the right to stay! I am the task force of the group that freed the cyborgs and the duly appointed representative of the Interstellar Armed Forces. These two were removed from my custody, and that woman is wanted for questioning for hacking the IAF military software."

Phaedra looked intrigued. "I didn't hear about this. What did you do?"

"Nothing. He's chasing the wrong comet if he thinks I had anything to do with it. I'm a simple cargo jockey."

"It was you," Heath spoke this time. "Or was it these alien weapons with you?"

Hezza stared the officer down. "How many times do I have to tell you, Kalan and Fyr'enth are not alien weapons. They're not weapons at all. They're living beings!"

Hezza watched as Heath transformed from a polished officer into a frothing madwoman.

"Liar!" the woman shrieked. "Betrayer! You are sleeping with humanity's enemy! They are a threat to humanity. We must resist before it's too late."

The colonel gawped at his first officer. "Rosalyn? What are you doing?"

"Don't you understand? This is what I told you about. This is the moment. We have to fight back and reclaim this galaxy for humanity."

Everyone in the room was watching the drama play out as if they'd bought tickets for this show. Hezza was distracted too, but then she saw it. The same cold-eyed look Heath had worn when she'd called her mates alien weapons the first time.

She reacted blindly, convinced that something terrible was about to happen.

Kalan and Fyr'enth must have seen the same thing she did because they both flared their wings, using them as shields to screen the others.

Only, she wasn't there anymore. She was running straight for Heath, determined to stop her from hurting someone she cared about.

Barrios grabbed at Heath, shouting incoherently as he tried to break her grip on her sidearm.

"Rosalyn, stop this! Stop!" Barrios shouted.

She kept going, fear for her mates pushing her just as hard as the nanotech in her body.

The weapon discharged, sending a sizzling blast of energy that zipped by Hezza's shoulder. Less than a second later, a flash of light passed her again, this time coming from behind. A rebound? Or had the shot been deflected by one of her mahoyen's wings. It slammed into Barrios's leg. He screamed and went down hard, leaving Heath standing alone.

Hezza dropped her shoulder and hit her in the midsection. They both crashed to the deck, but Hezza was on top, which gave her the advantage.

So did the nanotech.

She used both to push herself to her knees.

Heath tried shove her off and failed. "Bitch. You don't understand. If the empress died, they'd leave us alone!"

Hezza briefly considered explaining to the woman how wrong she was. But what would be the point?

"This is for calling my mates weapons," she snapped and then punched Heath square in the face.

Her hand went numb as she connected with Heath's nose. Something cracked, but she couldn't tell which of them was the source of the noise.

She used the last of her energy to take the weapon out of Heath's limp hand and toss it to one side.

Still kneeling on her rival's unconscious body, she twisted around to check on Fyr'enth, Kalan, and everyone else.

"Are you alright?" she demanded, fearing that they'd been hurt somehow.

"We are." Kalan rushed to her side, worry etched on his face. "Are you?"

"Me?" She had to think about that for a moment. That's when the pain finally registered. "I think I busted my hand."

Kalan cursed and wrapped his arms around her, lifting her to her feet while being careful not to jar her injured hand. "I take it back. You are not allowed to protect yourself anymore. We're taking over the job."

"Yes, we are," Fyr'enth agreed. "You told us trouble always seemed to find you. I think it's the other way around."

Her head swam, but she laughed and leaned against Kalan, trusting him to hold her up. "Maybe that's true. After all, I did find the two of you."

"Yes, you did, *zana*." Fyr'enth stroked her cheek softly.

"And now, we'll be with you until the end of the universe," Kalan said.

She liked the sound of that.

EPILOGUE

NANOTECH COULD DO MANY THINGS, but it couldn't block pain. Fortunately, she didn't have to suffer for long.

Once Barrios and Heath were in custody, Tyran personally escorted Hezza and her mates to the platform's medical center. Once there, a kind and very gentle healer gave her a dose of pain blocker that lasted just long enough for him to reset and mend the bones she'd fractured when she knocked Heath unconscious.

Despite the damage to her hand, she'd come out of the fight better off than the lieutenant commander. The mentally unstable and soon-to-be-court-martialed female was back on the *Bright Arrow* for treatment of a concussion and broken nose.

Barrios had survived his injuries, too. Though Hezza doubted his pride would ever fully recover.

The prince had agreed to both he and Heath being placed into IAF custody because the colony didn't have the facilities to hold a prisoner. At least, not yet. The way things were going, they'd need to address that issue soon.

Fyr'enth and Kalan had stayed with her during her treatment, which hadn't taken very long at all. Vardarian healing was definitely a step above anything humanity had to offer. Or maybe she just couldn't afford what a corporation would charge for that kind of treatment.

In the aftermath of the meeting, answers were in short supply. So instead of waiting around for information that might take days, she let her mates take her back to the *Gambit* to rest.

That had been two days ago.

Now they were back in that same meeting room, having a very different discussion than the one they'd had the last time.

For one thing, the leadership council of Haven wasn't here this time. Nor were any representatives from the IAF. It was just Hezza and her mates talking with Tyran, Braxon, Phaedra, and Neha.

"They want to go back to Vardaria with you?" Fyr'enth asked the empress.

"They do." Neha actually smiled as she spoke. "They will be treated with respect and kindness. I promise."

While she had been resting, the other cyborgs from Orio Station had been roused from their cryo-pods. Most of them had chosen to stay on Haven, at least for now, but two of them wanted to go with Neha to see the homeworld they'd never known.

"They're members of the imperial family. No one will dare to say anything," Neha assured them.

"Even if they're thinking it," Tyran said. He wasn't as comfortable with the idea as his sister, but he wouldn't stop the pair of cyborgs from making the trip if that was what they wanted.

"It will be alright, brother. I've talked to mother, and we think this is the best way forward. Until the other day, I didn't realize...." She sighed and scrubbed a hand across her face. "I erred. I didn't want to see how deep the rot had set in. When that female started saying those terrible things, I realized they were variations of the same thing some of my advisors have said. It made me see things differently."

"I'm glad you see it now," Phaedra said, her voice soft and comforting for once. "We can change things. Make them better. I want my daughter to grow up in a galaxy where she is valued for what she can do, not the purity of her bloodline."

Neha nodded. "I want that too. And I need to apologize to you, Phaedra. I haven't been fair to you. Or to you, Braxon." The empress smiled at her brother's *anrik*.

"I thought I was making good choices, but I wasn't making choices at all. I was letting other people tell me what I should do without asking why they wanted it that way."

Hezza nodded but stayed quiet. It didn't feel like Neha was done talking yet.

"I've accepted that my empire is rotting from the inside. As Phaedra says, we have to change things. My father believed this infection would heal itself in time. My brother once told me that change would only come if we cut out the rot and encouraged new ideas to grow in its place. I should have listened to you, Tyran. Instead, I listened to those who told me what I wanted to hear. Again, I am sorry."

She gave her brother a small smile. "I think I'm going to be saying that a great deal in the near future. I have a lot to answer for."

"Don't apologize too much. Some will take that as a sign of weakness instead of your intent to make amends. And since I'm handing out advice, here's some more. Never trust anyone who tells you what to think without giving you a good reason why," Hezza said.

"Good advice. I'll try to remember that when I return home." Neha looked at her with curiosity. "What about you? Where will you go now?"

"For now, we'll stay here. I want to be nearby when we finally find out what was going on between Barrios and Heath."

Phaedra grinned. "Didn't you hear? He's told the investigators everything. Not that there's much to tell. He's the one who had trackers placed on both the *Bat* and the *Gambit*. He didn't trust any of you not to ruin his chance for accolades."

"And Heath?" This was news to Hezza, and she wanted to hear the details. Talking about her future plans could wait.

"She was stringing him along. They weren't romantically involved. Barrios was adamant about that. He thought he was mentoring a rising star, someone he could use to elevate his own career. It didn't hurt that she had corporate connections and kept hinting she could get him a private contract once he was done with active service."

"He mentored her yet somehow failed to notice she had fanatical views on humanity's place in the universe?" Hezza snorted. "That's an impressive level of selective blindness."

"Turns out, she's not the only one. The IAF is going to be busy cleaning their own house for a while." Phaedra glanced over at Neha. "Your empire isn't the only one with problems."

"Apparently not." Neha nodded and then turned the conversation back to Hezza. "What other plans do you have?"

"Like I said, we'll stay here for a while. Fyr and Kal want to get to know the colonists and learn more from both sides of their heritage. Then? I guess I go back to work." She smiled at her mates. "But this time, I won't be doing it alone."

"Together. Always," Kalan said.

"Always," Fyr'enth echoed his brother.

"If that's your plan, I have an offer for you. It's time to increase our ties to this part of the galaxy. That means increasing trade. We would like to offer you a *chalocha*."

"I'm sorry, I don't have a translator implanted yet. That's something else I'll get done before we leave."

"Of course. I think the word translates to something like an imperial charter. Your ship would have exclusive rights to certain trade goods. Over time, we'll expand the number of these available, but for the moment, you'd have the only one. Is this agreeable to you?"

Hezza whooped and nodded so hard she saw stars. "Hells yes, it is. Uh, I mean, that's very agreeable to me. And very kind of you and Tyran."

She looked at her mates and smiled as she saw a whole new future unfolding for the three of them. "We're going to need a bigger ship."

Tyran nodded. "Of course. That would be part of the agreement."

A strange buzzing filled her head and made it impossible to think clearly. Had she heard that right? They were offering her a charter and a new ship?

While she floundered, Fyr'enth spoke up. "We accept the offer, but we have some requests." He held up one finger. "We'll need a cabin that can accommodate all three of us."

Kalan held up two fingers. "And the galley will need the best food dispenser on the market. One that makes pizza."

It was the deal of a lifetime. Two mates, one ship, and a lifetime supply of pizza.

And it was all hers.

***

Thank you for reading Her Alien Cyborgs.

I hope you enjoyed Hezza, Fyr'enth, and Kalan's story. Would you like to read a special bonus epilogue to this story? Sign up for my newsletter here: subscribepage.io/Bonuscontent

While this is the final book in the Haven Colony series,

fear not! In 2026 I will be launching a new series. The Drift: Defiance Station.
If you're looking for more stories like this one, I invite you to explore the other books in the Drift universe, which now Include Haven Colony, Nova Force and the original Drift series.

ABOUT THE AUTHOR

USA Today Bestselling author and writer of award-winning Sci-Fi and Paranormal Romance, Susan recently moved from the wilds of western Canada to the southern coast of Australia. These days she writes from her new home where her every word is scrutinized by her step-lizards and her coffee mug is kept full by her beloved husband.

To contact her about her books or to ask her about her new life in Australia, you can email her at susan@susanhayes.ca or find her at susanhayes.ca. If you'd prefer to stalk her from afar, you can sign up for her newsletter http://susanhayes.ca/susans-newsletter/